Weathering the Storm

Weathering the Storm

A Collection of Short Stories

by

Anne Bainbridge

BLUE POPPY PUBLISHING

Weathering the Storm © 2019 Anne Bainbridge

The right of Anne Bainbridge to be identified
as the author of this work has been asserted.

This is a work of fiction; all the characters, events, and settings are fictional or are used in a fictional way. Any similarity to any real persons, living or dead, and any similarity to businesses, places, or organisations, is entirely coincidental.

BLUE POPPY PUBLISHING

DEVON EX34 9HG

info@bluepoppypublishing.co.uk

ISBN-13 978-1-911438-61-8

1st Edition 2019

Dedication & Thanks

I'd like to thank Vera, Anna, Michael, Colin,
Sophia, and Olli for all your help.

Thanks also to the South Molton Writing Group
for their inspiration and support.

Contents

Weathering the Storm 1

A Little Rebellion 8

Madison 17

Generosity 22

Island 34

The Crofter's Wife 37

Witness 45

Here's Looking at You, Kid 52

Miriam 61

Peculiar Pair 66

Meg 69

Fen Meadow 78

The Summer Fair 87

Stalemate 91

Moving On 99

The Wine Taster 107

Vera 113

Weathering the Storm

It was generally considered throughout the fairground community, that Madam Zelda was losing her touch. But no one, not even the Mighty Merlyn, her friend and sometimes comforter could say exactly what her 'touch' had lost. When the morning sun hit the mirrored walls in her showman's trailer, shedding a golden light on the polished floor and a prism of colour shot through the crystal vase of pink peonies and Rosea Lavender, it was hard to see that anything was amiss. But something, a little something was not quite right. As Madam Zelda attended to her appearance with the artistry and precision of a master gem cutter, transforming a rough diamond into an exquisite jewel, her finely groomed figure gave no indication that anything was not as it should be. She continued to rise at first light and take to her bed a few minutes before midnight, allowing sufficient time to be comfortably settled between silk sheets before the grandmother clock chimed twelve and heralded a time of dreams.

So what was it, when daily routine and ardent attention to her appearance continued with such normality, that led Madam Zelda's friends to meet in secret on the one day of the week they knew the fortune teller would be forty miles away in search of a new crystal ball?

"She's not herself," said one.

"She's lost her touch," said another.

"It's in her eyes" Merlyn sighed, "It's as if she no longer sees us."

And as one, the men and women of the travelling fair nodded in agreement, that Merlyn who knew her best of all, was quite right and that in the eyes of Madam Zelda they had indeed become invisible.

How wrong they were.

Madam Zelda was seeing her fairground friends quite clearly for the first time and it was causing her to feel uncommonly ill at ease. They were also wrong about her search for a new crystal ball. How that story spread we will never know but Madam Zelda, although many miles away on the day of their clandestine gathering was in reality on her way to visit her oldest friend Kathleen Rafferty, who was lying in a hospital bed waiting for her luck to change.

As often happens between old friends, it wasn't out of the ordinary that Madam Zelda should have looked at the screen on her mobile phone only to see Kathleen's name appear at precisely the same moment she was going to call her. The coincidence of both women thinking of communicating at the same time, confirmed Madam Zelda's belief, that Kathleen Rafferty was the one person in the world in whom she could confide. But on hearing that her friend was undergoing tests for a condition which Kathleen had glibly referred to as a 'dicky' heart, had distressed Madam Zelda on several accounts. First and foremost she was concerned for her friend's wellbeing. There was also disappointment. She felt she could no longer burden her sick friend with her own troubles. Of course if the illness turned out to be more than a dicky heart, Madam Zelda's anxiety for the future would be confirmed.

How wrong she was.

For as luck would have it by the time she reached the hospital ward, her old friend gave every impression of being in the pink and was looking forward to going home sometime very soon. The friends looked at one another and disregarding all need for small talk of journeys or heaviness of the weather Kathleen asked outright, "What's on your mind Jess?" It had been a long time since anyone had called Madam Zelda, Jess. Only Merlyn, who occasionally whispered her name when she switched her silk sheets for his quilted eiderdown, was granted such a privilege. She liked being Jess. Jess had fun. Jess could let her guard down. Jess could confide in her old friend and so, without so much as a 'How are you?' she told Kathleen Rafferty what was on her mind.

As is so often the way when confidences are revealed she began with a confession. So, with steady breath, Jess let it be known that unknown to her fairground friends, she, unlike her mother and grandmother, did not have the gift of scrying; Madam Zelda could no more foretell the future using a crystal ball than fly to the moon. With this great weight off her chest, Jess now felt a need to mention that she didn't consider herself to be a complete fraud because she could, without question, see through people. She could, as they say, read them, and having taken their money she told them what they needed to know. And those who chose to cross her hand with silver invariably profited from what she had to say. To the struggling she offered strength, to the lost she showed direction and to those whose confidence had been squeezed away by misfortune she endeavoured to restore their self-belief. And now with recognition of her own worth she was ready to proceed; she was ready to tell her friend all that had happened on the last night of Pewsey Fair.

The inclement night had brought more than usual into Madam Zelda's tent. Among the anxious and the eager waiting to have their fortune told there were the faithful fairground fans willing to part with their money in return for a good story to tell the following day. The last person to enter the tent that night, like many of the sodden souls before her, wanted only shelter from the storm. The child, and yes she was no more than a girl, was already sitting at the table when a flash of lightening blazed all around and Madam Zelda's eyes were caught in the light of the child's moonstone earrings. And in that fleeting moment she saw, in the pearly veil of stones, her younger self. She saw her own moonstone earrings, as ancient as the moon, glisten against her own perfect skin, she saw the mother of pearl comb holding back her dark, unruly hair. She saw her red flamenco skirt and white chemise. She saw her lost youth.

So perhaps it is no wonder that, when a deafening clap of thunder cracked directly overhead, shaking the very fabric of both tent and Madam Zelda's mind, she saw before her the girl in red and white, with perfect skin and dark unruly hair, aging before her eyes until there was nothing left but dust. In the quiet and calm that followed, Madam Zelda, so to speak, returned to earth.

The girl with the moonstone earrings, unaware of the fortune teller's vision, gladly accepted a refund believing without question that the forces of nature had clouded the crystal ball and that there would no more fortune telling that night. But Madam Zelda could not put what she had seen from her mind. Nor could she shake off a terrible sense of foreboding and disquiet that hung heavily over her and upon those around her. Where once she saw smiles, she now only saw frowns. Where once she heard laughter, she now heard grumbles and complaints. This and an awful lot of dust was what had been on her mind since the night of the storm.

Sitting by her friend's bedside having talked things through (a simple practice that has greater effect than the words might lead you to believe) a new light was rising within Madam Zelda.

They sat in comfortable silence, before Kathleen Rafferty, also known as Madam Belrose asked "So how do you feel now?"

"Better," Jess replied, "What about you?"

"I'm fine and as soon as they fit me up with a stent I'll be as right as rain."

The two women talked for a while about the heaviness of the weather and what constituted a moderate amount of chocolate in a healthy diet. They talked of tea leaves, tarot cards and palms; as for the art of scrying they thought that there was probably no need for a crystal ball to see all there was to be seen. They did however agree that they shed a beautiful light.

Meanwhile back on the camp site it had been decided, that as Madam Zelda was definitely not 'herself' and the right and sensible thing to do would be for someone to ask if something was troubling her. Merlyn was that someone.

The strong man sat in his caravan searching for words.

But Mighty Merlyn had no need to worry, for when, later that evening Madam Zelda let herself into his trailer and brushed her hand over his quilted eiderdown, he only had to whisper 'Jess', and he knew that Madam Zelda had by no means lost her magic touch.

A Little Rebellion

Tanja, the Bulgarian au pair was concentrating on making the children's packed lunches and trying to remember, which twin wanted ham sandwiches and which one tuna and mayonnaise. All the while, the eldest child, Abigail was remonstrating because Tanja had put peach yoghurt in her lunch box instead of a strawberry one and "didn't the stupid woman know that peaches made her feel sick?" All of which was making it increasingly difficult for the 'put upon' au pair to think clearly. It wasn't helped by Julia, her employer, and mother of the 'hard to please' children firing questions and instructions at her every five seconds.

"Tanja, be a poppet and empty the dishwasher... Oh and don't forget the recycling bin, there's a darling." Tanya bit her lip and answered with a polite "Okay!" She always emptied the dishwasher before she walked the three badly behaved children to school and not once had she forgotten to put the recycle bin out. She couldn't decide whether her employer repeated herself because she thought all foreigners were stupid, or that she simply liked the sound of her own sonorous voice; the same booming voice that was now demanding the Lord's attention.

"Dear God. It must be here somewhere." Tanja looked on nervously as Julia checked the top of the fridge, the cutlery drawer and inside the bread bin for the manila envelope that she had scribbled the day's shopping list on only a few minutes earlier.

Checking her watch Julia turned her attention back to Tanja, "Oh, it doesn't matter. Just buy something for tea. There's money in the fruit bowl and, before I forget, can you pop into the newsagents and find a nice birthday card for my mother? That would be a great help. Now I must dash! Bye, bye my sweeties, love you. Be good!" Julia planted a kiss on each of her children's heads and headed for the door. She hesitated for a moment, conscious that there was something she had forgotten. When nothing came to mind she hurried out of the kitchen, picking up papers and car keys, believing that whatever it was she had failed to remember couldn't have been all that important; then left the house slamming the front door behind her.

No sooner had the VW Golf GTI pulled out of the drive, than Robin came thumping down the stairs. "Was that Julia leaving?" he shouted, to no one in particular and dashed down the hall, opened the front door, letting rip a thunderous "Damn!"

"Damn, damn, damn."

"Don't swear, Daddy!" piped up Abigail.

"I'm not swearing, but Daddy's feeling a bit unhappy because Mummy has forgotten that she was going to take him to the railway station this morning. Now he's going to have to drive there, spend half an hour trying to find somewhere to park, miss his train and then be late for his meeting. Damn!"

"It is a swear word daddy because when you say 'damn' it means you're damning someone to hell and..."

"Not now Abby." snapped Robin with immediate regret, but Abigail was already running up the stairs in a huff.

"Oh, hell." sighed Robin throwing his other two children a warning look just in case they decided to follow their sister's suit and reprimand him for blaspheming. He needn't have worried. The twins were happily spooning Cheerios into their mouths, while watching something loud on their iPads.

"You want coffee, Robin?" Tanja ventured to ask.

He was about to say something clever and cutting, when he had an idea. Ignoring Tanja's second attempt at the question, he exclaimed, "That's it! You can drive can't you? You can take me to the station and have my car for the day. It will save you the walk to school. Come on boys, get your skates on."

Before Tanja could reply Robin was shouting to Abby, promising to buy her something special on Saturday, if she got into the car immediately.

"Can we have something too?" chorused the boys." Yes, yes, come on Tanja, what are you waiting for?"

"I not know how drive car."

"Oh you'll get the hang of it; it's more or less the same as Julia's. I'll drive there and explain things to you as we go along. Just think you'll be able to have my car to do as you wish for the rest of the day. Now, come on. If we don't hang about I might make the 7:50."

Robin herded everyone into the car paying little attention to Tanja's babblings about not driving a car, dishwashers, and rubbish, and with further assurances of buying something very exciting at the weekend, managed to get all the three children strapped into their seats. He steered his BMW X3 out into the avenue and towards the morning traffic. The few parking spaces were already taken by the time

Robin jumped out of the car at the dropping-off bay. With the engine still running, he headed towards the station, leaving Tanja to climb into the driver's seat and work out what to do next. Why had Robin said his BMW was more or less the same as Julia's VW? Tanja had never driven Julia's car. She wasn't even convinced she was insured to drive either vehicle.

When Robin and Julia had invited Tanja to be their au pair six months earlier they had clearly stated that she would have use of the family car, but, like many of the other promises made then, it had never happened. Now, when it suited, she was expected to drive an unfamiliar car, on an unfamiliar route, to the children's school and, even if their behaviour could be pretty awful, she had no desire to kill them. However, when Abigail suggested, somewhat unkindly, that Tanja didn't know how to drive, memories of speeding around Sofia's busy roads, in her father's unreliable Travant, came to mind. The Bulgarian au pair felt obliged to put the little girl, in her care, right.

"I drive like Vladimir Arabadzhiev, he famous Bulgarian Formula 1 driver."

With that, and trying to remember some of Robin's instructions, she fastened her seat belt, clenched the steering wheel, put the vehicle in gear, released the handbrake and pulled smoothly out into the exit lane. The slow-moving traffic allowed Tanja time to get used to driving on the left-hand side of the road and work out, which switches were what and, before she knew it, she felt as if she had been driving a BMW for ever. She parked perfectly, near the school gates, and watched the children line up in the playground, under the watchful eyes of the classroom teachers before driving back to the house, to the dishwasher and the recycling bin.

She wiped the sticky surfaces, washed the breakfast dishes by hand and took a lasagne out of the freezer, because there was no money in the fruit bowl to buy food for tea. She looked at the daily 'to do' list fixed to the fridge door with a 'Disney World' magnet.. Disney World, that was another broken promise and instead of the expected three weeks in Florida, Tanja had been lent to another family with a newborn baby, a toddler in nappies and a seven-year-old who enjoyed playing in her father's workshop that housed all kinds of machinery, all of which were covered in oil. Disney World would have been nice. A holiday would be nice 'to be by the waters lovely' would have been perfect. She shut her eyes and childhood holidays by the Black Sea drifted into her mind, and she longed for the smell and taste of salt, she longed for sunny days, blue, blue skies and glistening white sand. But mostly she longed for home.

Her mobile phone bleeped. It was a text from Julia.

> can u collect coat from cleaners ticket in one of kitchen drawers xx

Tanja didn't reply, but instead switched off her phone, went into the playroom and having stepped around a scalextric set, model railway, doll's house, three boxes of Lego, a large screen television and an indoor wigwam, sat herself at Abigail's computer. It took Tanja less than ten minutes to find, purchase and print out a bus ticket for Sofia that was leaving Victoria Coach station at ten o'clock that very evening. The ticket had cost €89. The train fare to London would probably cost twice that amount but the one commitment Robin and Julia had kept was that they had paid her; it wasn't a lot but enough money to get home. That of course was the easy part. She switched her phone back on. There were two more messages from Julia:

> found shopping list need coffee urgent xx

followed by

> must be decaf xx

Tanja scrolled down the list of contacts until she came to Julia's Mother's name and rang the number hoping that it wouldn't go through to her answer machine. Tanja instinctively pulled the telephone away from her ear as the familiar, friendly voice boomed "Hello Margery Miller speaking?"

"Hello Mrs Miller, it Tanja, I sick, please you take children from school today."

"Who's this?"

"Tanja, Julia au pair I sick. Please you take children from school today?"

"Oh Tanja dear, how are you?"

"I sick. Please you take children from school today."

"You want me to collect the children from school is that it?"

"Yes, you take."

"Yes, yes alright I take children from school.

"Thank you Mrs Miller. You very kind"

"Okay dear."

Tanya thanked Julia's mother one more time and switched off her phone before anything more could be said. She hadn't really told a lie, she was sick, she was home sick. She liked Mrs Miller and hearing her voice made Tanja stop and think. She could sacrifice the bus ticket and just tell Julia and Robin, how she longed to go home as soon as possible. They were reasonable people weren't they?

Tanja sprinted up the stairs, packed her bags and for the second time that day, she found herself driving towards the railway station where she parked the BMW in the nearest pay and display car park, before catching the midday train to Waterloo.

Later that day, sitting in St James Park she sent Robin a text:

> i go home your car at gaydon steet car park keys up exhaust pipe.

Within seconds a text flashed on her screen

> u r joking

Tanja pressed delete, he'd got the message. Tanja, the no-longer 'put upon' Bulgarian, was thinking clearly. She had one more text to send, before setting off for Victoria Coach station and the fourteen-hour journey home.

> julia it tanja, i sick i go home u take coat from cleaners u buy coffee and card for mother and strawberry yogurt for Abigail she not like peach xx

Madison

It was already five to three and the fracture clinic was full. A three o'clock appointment was out of the question as was the likelihood of missing the rush hour on the way home. Knowing that there was nothing to be done, Luca Spacone eased himself into a high-backed, powder blue, vinyl chair and resigned himself to a long wait.

Luca picked up a copy of Reader's Choice and flicked through the not so glossy magazine in hope of finding something remotely interesting to read, that would help to pass the time. Within seconds he came across a headline that caught his attention.

MADISON: I SHOULD HAVE BEEN BORN A WOMAN.

Luca was enthralled by the article about a former, hard-nosed security guard now called Madison who, after a year into transition, was learning how to cope with living as a woman. He was just about to turn the page, when a piercing alarm rang through the waiting room and all eyes focused on the flashing light above the disabled toilet. Two nurses and an orderly rushed towards the door, while those immobilised by plaster casts could do nothing more than watch the drama unfold.

The excitement was cut short when a well-built woman with her neck in a brace and a face as red as her woolly hat, stepped through the toilet door and sheepishly confessed to pulling the emergency cord by mistake. The penetrating ring was swiftly silenced by the efficient orderly. The readers returned to their reading, the 'fidgets' continued to fidget while others kept their eye on the clock on the wall.

As for Luca, the ear-splitting sound of the alarm bell had transported his mind elsewhere. He was no longer in the waiting room but back at school with his friend Mai. He could see Mai clearly. It was Monday morning. He always hated Mondays; a punishing PE lesson first thing, the rest of the day spent avoiding the classroom bully and five whole days of school before the weekend.

The two friends were standing on the playing field waiting for their names to be called out, but they were as always the last to be picked for the rounders team. "Right" said Miss Jackson irritably, "Mai you take a red band and Luca Spacone you join the blue team and Michael if I have one more word out of you, you'll be sitting on the bench."

Luca avoided Michael Maguire's pale green eyes and took his place at the back of the line and prayed for rain.

The sun had shone throughout. And after yet another torturous P.E. lesson Luca changed into his school uniform as quickly a possible and hid in the 'disabled' toilet during break to avoid the humiliating teasing and painful kicking that he was sure to receive for loosing the game. It wouldn't be the first time Michael had hissed in his ear "I'll get you for this Spacko." And there was one thing Luca knew for sure about Michael Maguire was that he was a boy who always kept his word.

Luca double checked that the door was locked and wept. He was a Spacko, a Spacko hiding in a Spacko loo. He hated P.E. he hated school and most of all he hated himself.

"Don't take any notice of him," Mai had said but it was difficult to ignore someone who pushed, shoved, and punched you at every opportunity they could get. And Miss Jackson never helped, how many times did she threaten to put Michael on the bench, loads, and how many times did he sit on the bench, never; even when he was caught red-handed bashing Luca around the head with the rounders bat Miss

Jackson had believed Michael when he'd said it was an accident.

Miss Jackson had tried to be kind the day she found Luca sobbing in the book corner but when he'd been unable to tell her what was wrong she had told him to dry his eyes and stop being an attention seeker.

The problem was that Luca didn't know what was wrong with him. He just knew that what he felt inside, didn't fit the reflection he could now see in the mirror on the opposite wall.

He sat on the toilet and wondered what would happen if he pulled the red emergency cord. Alarm bells would ring, and help would come. If only, he thought, he had a cord inside his head he could pull. He needed someone to comfort him, he needed someone to say, "It's okay Luca, we're here. How can we help?" But all he could hear was familiar voices nearing the toilet door. Darren Parker, Michael's mealy-mouthed sidekick was speaking, "Yeah, and I bet he's in with the girls having his hair curled".

"Yeah or maybe…" laughed Maguire; suddenly bashing on the disabled door, "He's in here."

The sound of Michael Maguire's joyless laugh was so angry, so rancorous that, for the briefest moment, Luca had feared for his life and without further thought he had reached out and pulled the red cord.

A child's shrill cry from one of the consultants' rooms brought Luca back to the present. He was once again sitting in the waiting room, clutching the magazine, but his mind was fixed in the past. He tried to recall what had happened after he had pulled the emergency cord. He thought he could remember, but maybe it was what he had been told by his mother, that it was Eric, the curmudgeonly caretaker, who had found him curled into a ball between the broken-down lifting sling and the stinking lost property box. Eric had, with unexpected gentleness, taken him to the Headmistress's office.

Michael left the school because, according to Miss Jackson, he had certain issues and the bullying had stopped abruptly. Darren Parker even wanted to be his friend, but it took Luca years to realise that there was nothing wrong with him. He just preferred the company of girls and disliked sport, particularly those games that involved playing on the same team as Michael Maguire.

Michael Maguire, Maguire, Maguire… He hadn't thought about him for ages but now he couldn't get that name out of his head. Maguire had been on his mind even before the woman in the red hat had set off the alarm.

And then it hit him, bells rang Madison Maguire. Fifteen years older but there was no mistaking those pale green eyes.

Generosity

The quality of being kind and understanding, liberal in giving or sharing; unselfish; free from meanness or smallness of mind or character. Such is generosity of spirit and the following story begins in buoyant mood as the generous staff and supporters of Fernley General Hospital celebrate the opening of a new Special Care Baby Unit and Family Room. Chloe and Jane are among those present who are balancing canapés and ham sandwiches on paper plates while sipping a complementary glass of wine.

Chloe's choice is the white; Jane's red. Chloe licks her fingers clean Jane uses a napkin. The women have met once before but they don't know each other. Neither do they know that in less than twenty-four hours after the ribbon has been snipped they will be sitting in a quiet café not daring to catch each other's eye and hoping beyond hope that the words of St.

Luke "Give, and it will be given to you." would as they say come home to roost! But, that is almost the end of the tale; first we must return to the evening where there is cause for great celebration.

* * * * *

The Senior Paediatric Intensive Care Nurse's speech was met with a gentle clap and an occasional "Hear, hear" as she outlined the many benefits the SCBU and family room would bring. But it was her final words that received the greatest applause:

"It's often the little things which make such a big difference. It is thanks to our supporters who have worked so hard to raise money, and to those who have made such generous donations, that we have been able to completely refurbish the family room and provide a comfortable place for friends and relatives to stay."

The Mayor, looking exceedingly dapper in his official robes, added a few more kind words and duly snipped the pink and blue ribbon that hung across the entrance to the unit. Chloe could hardly believe the moment had come. She had worked tirelessly organising coffee mornings, bread and soup lunches, pub quizzes and countless raffles. Fundraising had taken up a substantial amount of her time and energy, so when an invitation to the grand opening dropped on her doormat her sense of joy was only surpassed by an overwhelming feeling of being valued. And now here she was, and she was in high spirits. Chloe knew most of the fundraisers and recognized a few of the staff but there was one woman whom she thought she knew but couldn't place and it was bugging her. She knew that she knew her from somewhere but for the life of her she couldn't remember where. She tried thinking of cafés, shops, and offices where she might have seen her but drew a blank. Chloe thought she might have come across the woman at work. But, hard as she tried, she couldn't picture the woman with a cat, a dog, a budgie, or a Vietnamese Pot-bellied pig.

Of course the sensible thing to do would be to go and talk to her. But looking again she noticed the expensive Jaeger suit and the Harvey Nichol's shoes and sensing a coolness in the woman's manner Chloe decided that the Lady in Jaeger looked rather 'stand-offish' and would most likely not want to speak to her; so putting all such thoughts from her mind looked around for a second glass of wine and another ham sandwich. Then it happened; 'stand-offish' of course and it came to her in a flash. The Lady in Jaeger was in the unit when Ben, her middle child was born. It was a long time ago, but Chloe felt certain that it was the same person.

Ben had been a breech birth and whisked away to an incubator while Chloe had slept in a pethidine haze for twenty-four hours. As soon as she could walk she had made her way to the special care unit where she had lowered herself gingerly onto a hard plastic chair and waited for the moment she could hold her son. There were three babies in the unit: Ben, a baby girl Heidi, and another boy with 'no name' and a surname written on the side of the incubator. Heidi's mum was no more than a girl herself and was always glad of Chloe's company but 'no name's' mother was much older and didn't want to talk preferring to read instead; stand offish.

Well she didn't have a book now, so Chloe decided to take a chance and stepping through the crowd she touched the woman lightly on her arm and spoke in her best receptionist's voice.

"Hello, my name's Chloe Barnes I was wondering if we'd met before."

The woman met Chloe's eye, but when she gave no immediate reply Chloe continued, "I had a baby here twenty years ago." adding, as if it might stir the woman's memory, "He was breech."

Before the other woman could make any comment Chloe continued slightly faster than she'd intended "And you look like very much like of one of the mothers, so I thought maybe …"

She paused for a moment before taking a step backwards "Sorry, I'm probably mistaken but they do say everyone has a double - don't they?"

Jane looked at Chloe but didn't recognise her. She didn't think she knew anyone who wore quite so much makeup but on the other hand she couldn't be sure that they hadn't met. "I'm sorry your face isn't familiar, but my son was born here so I have always liked to support the hospital; possibility you have seen me here before."

Seeing the rather childlike look of hope on the Chloe's face Jane added, "Andrew was born here twenty years ago."

As the words left her mouth Jane did remember. She remembered two women who chatted so easily. One of them was no more than a girl herself. She remembered the hard, plastic chairs. She remembered how she had felt so lonely. Her husband Gerry was fighting in Bosnia and her baby boy was fighting for his life while all she could do was sit and wait; sit and wait.

"Yes, yes I do remember. The little girl was called Heidi."

The two women talked; Chloe at length, Jane in brief. Chloe learned that Jane's husband Major Hursey had just been appointed Chairman of The Board of Trustees at the hospital and their only child Andrew was in his second year at Leeds, reading Mathematics.

Within minutes Jane seemed to know everything there was possibly to know about Chloe's family. Chloe was a receptionist at the vet's in Market Street. Her husband Tom was an electronics engineer who worked for BT and had recently had an operation and had subsequently had to give up the allotment because the strain of digging potatoes and pulling up carrots could undo all the good work that the 'amazing' Serbian surgeon had performed on Tom's ventral hernia. And then there were the children! The youngest Amy always had her head in a book and didn't seem interested in boys. She was in the sixth form studying English, History, and Sociology and wanted to be a primary school teacher. Her eldest daughter Lucy didn't know what she wanted to do but was at university in Birmingham completing an MA and enjoying the student life. Ben she said was the odd one out. Ben was no academic. But as Jane soon found out he had an apprenticeship with a stone mason and had recently excelled himself by winning The Stone Federation Trainee Mason of the Year Award. Chloe's chatter seemed endless and seeing an old friend of her husband's Jane was about to excuse herself when Chloe reached into her bag and passed Jane a newspaper cutting. It was a short article with a large photograph of a smiling Ben holding the cup he had won for the Trainee Mason of the Year. Even without her glasses Jane could see the likeness. She was still staring at the picture when she heard her husband's voice "Are you all right darling you look quite pale?"

"Yes, I'm fine thank you. A glass of water would be nice" and glancing at Chloe added "Gerry could you possibly bring two glasses?" Jane had seen the photo of Ben. Chloe had seen Major Hursey in the flesh. There was no mistaking the likeness.

The women exchanged telephone numbers and email addresses and arranged to meet the following day.

*****

There were only two other customers in the café, an elderly gentleman reading a newspaper and a scruffy student highlighting words on even scruffier pieces of A4 paper. Jane was pleased that neither of them looked up and, indicating to the waitress that she was waiting for someone, she sat at a table in the far corner facing the door. She was early, but she had been up since five and had to get out of the house before Gerry got up. She had left a note on the kitchen table.

'Lovely morning. Thought I'd catch the market before it gets too busy. Back for lunch'.

It wasn't a lie, but it is what she hadn't told him that bothered her. Why hadn't she said something last night? She didn't know the answer to that or any of the other questions that were spinning around inside her head. All she knew was the boy Ben had to be her son. When she had looked at the face in the newspaper all she had seen was her once youthful husband; his dark wavy hair, square chin, and cool blue eyes.

She looked up at the clock. It was still early but a dreadful thought came into her head. Supposing the woman wasn't coming and at this moment she and her husband were sitting in a solicitor's office seeking advice, demanding compensation, demanding the return of their son. Jane recalled a case in the papers recently where babies had been switched at birth and the French clinic had paid out €1.8 million in damages. Although the parents had raised concerns that they had been given the wrong baby at the clinic, they ended up taking the children home. When the girls were ten DNA tests revealed that they had indeed, unwittingly, been handed the wrong infant. Neither family had wanted to swap the girls back, but it had taken another decade for the case to be closed. Jane couldn't bear the idea of court cases, DNA tests, prying journalists; the publicity would be insufferable. Why had that woman spoken to her and where was she? Where was Chloe? Hadn't Jane made it clear last night that they needed to talk?

A tiny bell tinkled as the door opened. Chloe caught sight of Jane's angry face in the corner of the room and wanted to turn and walk away but it was too late the woman had seen her.

They sat in silence waiting for the coffee to arrive. Chloe watched closely as Jane removed a large envelop from her bag and slid it across the table. She hesitated in taking it, for fear of finding records, legal documents, papers that would make Ben no longer hers. She slowly lifted the flap and pulled out a photograph, a photograph of Andrew. "Oh!" she gasped "he's lovely." There was no resemblance to her husband Tom, but she could see her daughter Amy in him, and everyone said Amy looked like her. Chloe was looking at her son. She slipped the photograph back in to the envelop and finally managed to speak "He looks a little like my youngest daughter."

"And you" replied Jane relieved by the warmth in the other woman's voice.

The coffees came and the women talked. After their second cup of coffee they decided to have lunch. Jane phoned her husband and explained that she had met a friend and wouldn't be home until later. Chloe could hear the "*Right Ho.*" from where she was sitting. The two women continued to talk. By the time the food arrived both women were in agreement that the mix up at the hospital must have happened in the early hours of the morning. They both recalled the maternity unit being busy and talk of understaffing. Their babies had been born within ten minutes of each other. Andrew was delivered by emergency caesarean section. Ben had been breech and the midwife had had to work swiftly to remove the cord from his neck. The same night Heidi had been delivered five weeks prematurely. Chloe and Jane speculated that after a long shift and in the urgent need to connect tubes and regulate the oxygen supply the nurse responsible had not written out the name tags immediately and when she came to do it later the mistake had occurred. Neither woman believed there was any call for the hospital to be investigated and hopefully there would be no need for any DNA tests, but they agreed that their families should be told. Telling the truth was the right thing to do.

They ate in silence. Jane's fears about suing the hospital were abated; apart from the all the fuss, it would have put her husband Gerry in an awkward position now that he was chairman of the board. But it was Gerry's health that gave her cause for most concern. At forty-two, after eighteen years of army service her husband had been eligible for Early Departure Payments and a tax-free lump sum of money, so they had been able to live very comfortably. It had also given him time to recover and face the world again. Having Andrew at thirty-eight, after years of trying to have a baby, should have been the happiest time of Jane's life but when Gerry came back from Bosnia and saw his son for the first time all he could do was cry. He had come home with a head reeling with such barbarous cruelty that talk of gallantry and the auspicious honour bestowed upon him by his superiors were lost in an all-consuming bloody nightmare. He had accepted the medal graciously, immediately hid it from sight and spent the next two years of his army career sat at a desk trying to forget.

Retirement had been good for her husband the nightmares became less frequent and he and Andrew spent hours together out on their boat; sometimes fishing but usually fixing and repairing and generally keeping the thing afloat. And when Andrew went to university Gerry gladly took up the position of Chairman of The Board of Trustees at Fernley General Hospital. He was known for keeping a clear head, always calm in the face of political shenanigans or financial troubles, but, as Jane knew all too well, anxiety clouded his all too fragile mind when anything, no matter how small, jeopardised the happiness and welfare of his family. Jane was just contemplating the awful reality of telling her husband the truth about Andrew's parentage when Chloe interrupted her thoughts with a question that added panic to her own troubled mind.

"Are there any inherent illnesses in your family?"

The question slithered and pounded over and over again inside her head. Did she mean mental health? Was Chloe reading her mind? Poor old Gerry's mental health condition was brought about by mankind's inherent appetite for war, not a faulty gene.

"Well" said Chloe "are there?" And not waiting for an answer but taking Jane's slight nod of the head to indicate 'no' she put the paper serviette she had been twisting around her fingers on the gingham table cloth, placed her hands flat on the table and let it out.

"The thing is I don't want anyone to know. I know it's the right thing to do but if I hadn't spoken to you last night we'd be none the wiser. We could just keep it to ourselves." When no response came she continued, "As far as we know neither of us has anything nasty lurking in our medical history. And yes there is a great likeness between your husband and Ben but like I said when we first met they say everyone has a double and unless anyone knew about the babies being in the special care unit at the same time it wouldn't cross their minds to think they were father and son." Chloe stopped only a moment for breath before carrying on. "The one problem would be if Andrew fell for either of my girls. Then we'd have to say something. Pity they're not all gay! He's not gay is he?"

Jane reached across the table and placed her hands on top of Chloe's. "No he isn't gay, but he does have a steady girlfriend. They're very fond of one another. I think it's serious, she's a bit of maths wiz, like Andrew, and they enjoy messing about in boats."

"That's nice" said Chloe. "So what do you think?"

Jane gave Chloe's hands the slightest squeeze and replied, "I think we should do the wrong thing."

Island

Joseph looked through the window and saw the island in the distance. He hated this run; no matter how many times his family and friends tried to reassure him that he was doing something good, something constructive to alleviate the unremitting suffering, he knew in his heart it wasn't good enough.

The island had suffered the world's worst industrial disaster known to mankind; within days of the explosion, the young, the week and the very old had perished. Those strong enough to stand buried the dead and tended the sick. But with polluted waters, failing crops, and contaminated cattle, goodwill waned, and when the inevitable struggle to get hold of bottled water and preserved food escalated into violence and rioting, the one remaining newspaper didn't hesitate in calling it Civil War.

Joseph's government had been quick to supply aid to the islanders and offer asylum to the vulnerable and dispossessed; but the refugees, as they were seen in the eyes of many of his countrymen and women, were an unnecessary burden on public resources. Many argued that the tax payer's hard-earned money should be spent on their own kind and so, it had been agreed, by those wishing to remain in power, that just five hundred more children would be granted asylum and the opportunity of a future without sickness and pain.

As the days passed into months, the heartbreaking stories of futile escapes from the island no longer made headline news. People began to forget the devastation, the misery, that had befallen the island. They reasoned that things weren't that bad after all. Before too long International Aid would end and the cause and effects of the disaster would become a subject for discussion rather than action and Joseph would no longer have to make the harrowing, hated runs.

His pity for the islanders was unceasing but compassion wasn't enough to prevent him form looking forward to the day when he no longer had to fly over the upturned boats and rickety rafts; all on board lost to the raging seas. He looked forward to the day when he no longer had to turn his back on mothers begging him to smuggle their infants on board or discovering yet another body of a young man strapped to the bottom of his plane. He looked forward to shutting his eyes at night without seeing the empty desperate faces that followed him into his dreams.

But he was here today, and he was doing something constructive. He looked through the window and saw the island below and, with the camp in sight, he made his slow decent over the White Cliffs of Dover.

The Crofter's Wife

Kitty had kept up with the other three for over an hour but now she was beginning to tire and seeing the steep rise ahead she decided that she would wait at the bottom of the path and enjoy the view from a sitting position. The others were shading their eyes as they searched the cloudless sky for sight of a golden eagle but there was nothing but blue beyond the purple landscape.

"Let's go, shouldn't take more than half an hour to get to the top," urged Robby.

Kitty spread her cagoule over the springy heather.

"You go ahead. I'll wait for you here. I'll be okay; I just need to rest,"

Sweet, kind, generous Carol, although, as eager as the others to continue the climb, without a second thought offered to stay behind. "Just in case," she said, "You know!" It took all of Kitty's powers of persuasion to convince her friend to go with the others. She would be fine; there was an excellent signal on her mobile so if anything happened, and nothing was going to happen, she could get help. Even Robby the most enthusiastic bird watcher out of the four said he would he would stay but Kitty was emphatic; so respecting her wishes and twitching to get going, he handed Kitty a bag of toffees with a "Don't eat them all at once." Luke on the other hand simply double checked the signal on his phone before setting off with the others on their quest for what Kitty reasoned they were as likely to find as the Holy Grail.

She was on her second sweet and dearly wishing her cravings were healthier. Her mother had hankered for parsley when she had been carrying Kitty. She had even heard of women who craved chalk during their pregnancies. Unfortunately all Kitty fancied was anything sweet: cake, biscuits, pastries, puddings, Blackpool Rock; it didn't matter as long as there was plenty of sugar. Nonetheless, she was determined to keep fit so resisting a third toffee, she rose to her feet with the idea of following the others. But with one glance at the sheer track ahead she knew that it would be foolish to attempt the climb, so she turned instead and began walking along the path to her left. The Highlands were beautiful and as Kitty ambled along the narrow path she dreamed of living there with

Luke. She could see herself striding over the hills with a child on her shoulders. They would live in a simple stone and thatch cottage. It would have an inglenook fireplace with a bread oven; there would be a rocking chair, patchwork quilts on all the beds and wild flowers in jam jars on the kitchen window sill. It was funny how she and Luke both liked storing stuff in jam jars; anything from elastic bands to Mr Garcia's freshly ground Columbian coffee. But they would have wild flowers in their house in the hills and they would leave the city behind and live happily ever after.

The sight of a farm building no more than a hundred yards away snapped Kitty from her daydream and suddenly, for a second or two, she felt quite afraid. Where there was a barn there would be animals: and where there were animals there would be someone to care for them. Kitty had not expected, nor wanted, to meet anyone. Instinctively she moved her hands to her rounded belly but resisting the urge to turn back, walked on. Thrift, Heath Bedstraw, Yellow Rattle and Butter Wort paved a way to what Kitty could now see was a dilapidated Crofter's Cottage. Peering through a murky window she could just make out the shape of a table and a heavy chain hanging down in the fireplace. She stepped back and inspected the thatch for signs of a chimney pot but could only make out tufts of grass and a line of moss stretching across the ridge.

The midday sun was making her feel weary and feeling certain the cottage was empty Kitty lifted the iron latch and leaned against the door. It was stiff but with a little push she managed to squeeze through a gap and into the cool. She was inside. She was inside and she was an intruder. She let out an involuntary "Hello, hello! Is anyone at home? Can I come in?" She knew that it was a silly thing to say but was still relieved when there was no reply. There was nothing in the room that Kitty hadn't already seen through the window except, that is, a wooden rocking chair in the corner of the inglenook fireplace. Swishing away the dust with her scarf and testing its sturdiness she carefully lowered herself into the seat and began to gently rock to and fro. To and fro, glad to rest before returning to the others.

To and fro, she popped a toffee in her mouth and wondered how they were getting on. She knew that Carol's kind offer to stay with her, and Robbie's sweeties were their way of saying 'We're here for you. You may think you're fine, but you never know!' Only Luke had taken Kitty at her word; if she said she was going to be fine then she would be fine. But it wasn't for the first time recently that Kitty had longed for him to question her decisions, challenge her determination for independence and today more than ever she had wanted it to be him who had volunteered to keep her company. But of course Luke had believed her when she said she was fine because that's all he knew what to do. And now in the cool of the Crofter's Cottage her mood shifted into a darker place. Kitty had stopped laughing at women who joked that their husbands or partners, like all men, as they saw it, had Asperger's. Kevin and his model trains ho, ho. Roger and his radios ha, ha. Tom with his collection of old cigarette cards, ha hilarious ho.

But somehow it wasn't so funny with Luke; the man utterly obsessed with computer programming, excessively sensitive to certain sounds, uncomfortable with small talk and mystified by the nuances and subtleties of language. No, when Kitty thought about it there wasn't much to laugh about living with someone who really did have Asperger's Syndrome.

In the beginning none of these things seemed to matter in fact they were what had attracted her to him in the first place. It wouldn't have occurred to Luke that a woman couldn't be successful in industry and he had never once doubted Kitty's ability to run her own business. And with promises of never having to worry about her PC crashing because he could guarantee backing up every document and spread sheet from here to kingdom come she had been smitten.

But pregnancy had changed Kitty. She didn't give a fig for her computer or her mobile phone. She wanted so much more; she wanted her precious baby to breath in clean fresh air in a peaceful, distress and disaster free, safe wonderful world; in short she wanted a perfect place for their child to grow up in.

And if she couldn't have that, she wanted Luke to be like everyone else and not always believe her when she said she was fine. And as all thoughts of being fine, and not being fine, and of world peace, and parsley, and too much sugar twisted this way and that inside her mind she became aware that the cottage was no longer comfortably cool but disturbingly cold. Cold and miserable she cried out,

"Why, why does everything have to be so hard?"

And an answer came, "Because it is lass." And in that moment Kitty saw a figure standing in the light of the window; young and slender but drawn and terribly pale; the woman was holding an infant in her arms. She smiled briefly at her baby and then she was gone.

What tricks of the mind were going on in Kitty's head she didn't care to dwell on, but she had heard a woman's voice and seen the face of hardship. Kitty wondered how many times the woman had had to fetch water and dig potatoes to fill the pot that would have hung from the chain over the fire, how many mouths had she fed at the wooden table, how many hours had she sat where Kitty was sitting now: mending, darning, and repairing. Kitty imagined the long winter days, the unrelenting rain, the bad summers when the barley crop failed and trekking across the harsh landscape for supplies. Worst of all she could see a mother nursing a sick child when there was no doctor to be found for miles around. Yet, Kitty had also seen the woman smile and for the first time since her pregnancy, she understood that the future might be hard, but she was not going to be alone.

With one last look around the crofter's cottage she shut the door behind her and blinked up at the sky. And there it was the white tail, the long broad wings held in a shallow 'V'. There was no doubt Kitty was watching a golden eagle soar and glide overhead.

Had the crofter's wife seen the eagle? Kitty liked to think she had and so with fanciful thoughts and practical steps she made her way back down the path to meet the others.

* * * * *

She took one more toffee and handed the rest back to Robbie who was sticking a plaster on his blistered heel. Carol was boiling water on the primus stove and speculating on the chance of the weather holding and a return visit the following day. Luke was eagerly telling Kitty how he had figured out how to programme his smart phone to allow only her name and number to appear on his screen if his line was engaged. He had previously succeeded in removing the irritating little icon that indicated someone waiting on line, but Kitty's number was different; it was important that she could contact him without delay when the baby was on its way.

"I'll need a new password, at least six letters." said Luke

Kitty was listening but her thoughts were on a rocking chair she had seen for sale in the funny little second-hand shop tucked away behind the Thai restaurant near where they lived and the cut flowers outside the corner shop at the end of their road: roses, zinnias and snap dragons, daffodils, and daisies.

"I'll need a new pass word, at least seven letters, two higher case," said Luke

"Jam Jars" said Kitty "Jam Jars."

Witness

There were very few occasions when The Honourable Ms Hilary Ferguson (QC) left court with a spring in her step. But today, she was feeling unusually cheerful and rather than taking a taxi home she decided to make the best of the Indian summer and chose instead to walk along the three-mile tow path that would bring her out onto Burnham Street. Here she could catch the last bus back to the end of her road where she lived with her ginger cat, Rumpole, in a ramshackle Victorian house she had inherited from her father, The Right Honourable Justice Ferguson, two years ago to the day.

Judge Hils, as she was affectionately referred to in Chambers, acknowledged that her recent sense of well being was due in part to now being able to think fondly of her father and remember the intelligent, generous, good natured man he had once been, rather than the miserable old curmudgeon she had cared for during the last years of his life. She knew all too well it had been his illness that had made him so unpleasant; so vitriolic! Sadly, however, understanding why he had been like it hadn't prevented her from being hurt by the constant criticisms and relentless sarcastic gibes which by the end was his only form of communication.

Now, two years on, it only took a passing word, a glimpse of colour in a crowd, the distant sound of church bells or the screech of a gull to spark a fond memory of her beloved father; her father cycling along the tow path pretending to be drunk, her father playing cribbage for pennies and promising to buy Buckingham Palace with his winnings and of course, perhaps best of all, her father telling such thrilling bedtime stories; stories far too exciting to send a little Hilary to sleep. For what seemed hours after he had tiptoed out of the room she would lie in bed imagining herself a fearless pirate upon the high seas, a Cheyenne squaw riding bareback across the Wyoming plains, or a famous cosmonaut soaring into the night sky in search of creatures from outer space.

Finally being able to lay to rest all such thoughts of the ill-tempered old man her father had become was not the only reason for her being in high spirits. Something quite extraordinary had happened in court that day leaving The Honourable Ms Hilary Ferguson (QC) with plenty to think about.

There was nothing particularly exceptional about the case. It was yet another dreadful robbery with threat of violence. Yet another victim whose ambition in life was probably not to be stuck behind a counter in the early hours of the morning selling chocolate bars and packets crisps to night owls or for that matter having an iron bar smash through, what according to the manufacturer was, protective glass. Yet another young offender whose desire for a better existence would in some way come to pass if sentenced to spend time at Her Majesty's Pleasure; behind bars he would at least lie in a clean bed and eat three meals a day. No, the all too familiar case was not anything to celebrate. What had lightened the Judge's mood was one Mr Frederick Pugsley, witness for the prosecution.

Fred Pugsley had pulled up into the forecourt of Hardman's petrol station just in time to witness a tall slight figure wearing a balaclava and carrying a loaded plastic bag and what looked like a crow bar running back from the kiosk and climbing into the passenger seat of a Ford Fiesta. Fred caught a glimpse of the female driver whom he described later as 'a young woman with short blond hair' and who reminded him of Margi Clarke in her starring role in Blonde Fist. As the car swung to the left, Fred noticed the passenger remove his balaclava and for a brief second caught sight of a shaven headed thin faced man before the car screeched out of the garage into the dark night. The witness had made a written note of the make, model and registration number of the car and was also able to tell the police which direction the vehicle had taken. Alarm bells were still blaring as he reached the kiosk. The terrified cashier had locked the door and not wishing to cause the woman further distress Fred had walked back to his van and waited for the police to arrive.

It hadn't taken the police long to trace the owner of the vehicle to a flat twenty minutes' drive from the scene of the crime. By the time they had acquired a search warrant there was no cash to be found but they recovered ten packets of cigarettes, four 25g pouches of rolling tobacco and several chocolate bars stuffed in the bottom of a sleeping bag along with a pair of dirty socks and some used tissues. They also found Karl Hicky, a tall slight man with a shaven head and owner of the Ford Fiesta. Mr Hicky immediately professed his innocence and insisted that the car had been taken without his permission by one or other of the many occupants in the squalid flat. Despite his protests the young man was read his rights and taken away for further questing. His girlfriend, the young blonde, who did indeed, in the opinion of the WPC, bare an uncanny likeness to Margi Clark was later arrested and charged with aiding and abetting.

But today it was Karl Hicky, now with short dark hair and dressed in an ill-fitting suit, standing in the dock and the prosecution were fairly certain of a speedy conviction. They had, they felt, sufficient evidence but they knew all too well that under pressure of cross examination their eye witness might be drawn into admitting that he couldn't be absolutely sure of what he had seen. What the Prosecution hadn't anticipated, and the police had failed to ask, was 'what was the witness doing out at that time of night?'

Therefore when Fred Pugsley answered, "I was looking for UFOs," you could say Mr Jeremy Flanders Council for Defence thought all his Christmases had come at once.

Consequently when he slipped in a couple of wisecracks about space ships and little green men the jury started to enjoy themselves.

It was at this point, that Judge Hils decided it was time to intervene. But Fred Pugsley beat her to it. He faced the bench and addressed her directly

"My Lady, with your permission I would like to make a brief statement regarding the subject which is the cause of so much amusement."

This, you might say, was a first for The Honourable Ms Ferguson (QC) so hoping not to betray her surprise, agreed to his request with the proviso that he would have to be very brief. With a nod of thanks Fred made his statement to the court.

"For as long as I can remember I have been interested in astronomy and have spent many hours starring into the night sky, spellbound by Sirius, Venus, The Great Bear, Orion's Belt, excited by the sight of a comet, a shooting star, a satellite or space station passing overhead but I am also fascinated by things, objects, moving across the sky that I can't identify. Is that so terribly strange? If it is then mock me for swearing, as I did today, on the Bible, a book rich in miracles and celestial manifestations." The witness paused for a second and turning again to the bench, he gave Judge Hils the tiniest smile before saying, "That's all."

Hilary was still thinking about that smile when she realised that she had already reached the Double Locks and the sun had a disappeared behind the line of empty warehouses and high-rise flats. It hadn't been a nervous smile or a smirk but a genuine smile of thanks. So, what with that smile, his eloquent way of speaking, and his love of the night sky, when she had said, "Do you have any further question Mr Flanders?" what she was thinking was how very much she liked Fred Pugsley.

It was dark by the time she reached the stone arch bridge and the path that would bring her out onto Burnham Street. The rumble of traffic sounded deceptively far away, and the not so distant lights cast an orange glow in the sky only the crescent moon shone overhead; its reflection shimmering on the still water.

The sudden gargling call of a moorhen startled the judge and when a curious string of gold and silver lights blazed across the crest of the bridge her mind returned once more to the eloquent Fred Pugsley.

The Judge had no intention of ever trying to contact the witness and when it was time for summing up the case she would do so solely on the evidence presented. But Mr Frederick Pugsley witness for the prosecution had reminded her that there just might be someone out there who liked ginger cats and wouldn't mind sharing a ramshackle Victorian house with a woman who once imagined soaring into the night sky in search of creatures from outer space.

Here's Looking at You, Kid

Hannah had always loved films and the older they were the better.

So when, only three weeks after graduating with a BA in Creative Digital Media, she started working for the BFI as a Digital Restoration Artist she thought her happiness complete.

The job specification could have in reality only been executed efficiently by three people. But Hannah had ignored the list of *'you will be responsible fors'* and submitted an application based on the more manageable *'being able to dos'* which included: digitally restoring films using various software, quick to learn new software tools and be familiar with data-centric post-production techniques and workflows.

In truth she wasn't particularly interested in post-production but knew just enough to give a satisfactory answer when asked about it at interview.

It had been her infectious enthusiasm for the film industry and her willingness to sit in front of a screen for hours restoring endless reels of acetate that had sealed the job and with luck she would never have to think about data-centric post-production techniques ever again. No, restoring endless reels of acetate was what she had wanted and restoring endless reels of acetate was what she was being paid to do. Hannah was indeed completely happy. Until that is, Alex left her and then she was completely miserable. At first she thought it was about the job. He had said she was nothing more than a glorified cleaner; a remark she considered uncalled-for not to mention a little unkind, but she put it down to his own frustration at not securing a job, as he put it, befitting his qualifications. He was instead working in Starbuck's for eight hours a day where he plied coffee to, in his words, cake and caffeine junkies.

So what if it was a glorified cleaning job; she used state-of-the-art software rather than a bucket and mop but there was no reason to be so sniffy about being a cleaner. Her grandmother had polished other people's silver and dusted their china for years not to mention removing chewing gum from under school desks in the evening. "Kids!" she'd say, "Dirty little toads." but it was never said in anger; she took pride in her work. Hannah understood this but it seemed that pride in cleaning was something Alex didn't get.

He had also said the work was boring and to that she really had no answer. It was impossible to calculate how long each restoration took; everything depended on the extent of the damage. With twenty-five frames to a second and most films running for one hundred minutes, the rough answer was a very, very, very long time. It was true that she had to spend hours at a workstation examining each frame, looking for scratches and marks that had to be repaired, getting rid of flickers and stabilising images, but it was interesting work. It was demanding, but never dull, never boring and the joy of viewing the completed work gave Hannah what is often too casually said but in her case sincerely meant 'job satisfaction'.

"You love your work more than me." he had said the day he dumped her, leaving Hannah feeling dejected, guilty, and worthless.

What Alex should have said of course is, "I've been two-timing you for six months with a waitress at Starbuck's who has found out about you and threatened to use the coffee grinder to remove my testicles if I don't dump you forthwith." But of course he didn't say any of this and it was months before Hannah discovered the truth leaving her feeling more miserable, more worthless, and stupid to boot.

She began to spend more time at work. It hadn't been unusual for her to stay behind on the nights that Alex was 'working late' to watch one of her favourite films at her workstation. But now it was every evening and always the same film.

* * * * *

It was while snuggling up between her grandma and granddad on their squashy settee that she had first set eyes on Humphrey Bogart. Custard creams and 'The African Queen', such bliss! There were other gems: Fred Astaire and Ginger Rogers in 'Flying down to Rio', Clark Gable and Marilyn Munroe in 'The Misfits', 'Waterloo Bridge' with Vivien Leigh, and Robert Taylor. But a film starring Bogie was always a bonus. Hannah had no idea how many times she had watched 'Casablanca' and heard her grandma say at the end, "Aye well, it was probably for the best."

Weekends at her grandparents' house were always the same. Saturday morning her father would drop her off at their front door and pick her up the following evening from the same spot. Her lovely dad who worked tirelessly around his daughter's school day and every weekend ever since Hannah's mother had emptied a basket of clean clothes into a tapestry bag and walked out of the kitchen door where a man called Jake was waiting to drive her to an ashram in Glastonbury where she was going to 'find herself'.

Hannah couldn't remember much about her mother and hadn't missed her. Her father cooked, cleaned, bought her new clothes, drove her to parties and sleepovers, read her bedtime stories and patiently listened to her endless word-for-word accounts of what had happened at school: – *And then Miss Carter said if Megan didn't stop talking she would put her in a lunch detention and when Megan said she had a to go to the dentist after school and Miss Carter put her in an after-school detention for answering back…It's just so unfair.*

And now sitting at her work station, having just completed a recently acquired Richard Massingham short, instead of celebrating she was feeling that everything was just … *was just so unfair*! It wasn't only Alex she missed it was her grandparents too. How she longed to be small again, sitting in their front room with the heavy oak side-board where the video tapes all clearly marked in her granddad's neat handwriting were piled high alongside glass vases, sherry glasses, and the rabbit shaped jelly mould. She longed to hear her grandmother say, "Aye well, it was probably for the best."

But that wasn't going to happen; she wasn't small, and her grandparents were busy looking after the twins, the 'oh' so cute Martha and the adorable blue-eyed Sam and apple of her grandmother's eye. Hannah fed the coffee machine with random coins and tried not to think like a brat. She couldn't remember ever resenting her father remarrying and had never until now resented her half brother and sister. But, as the scalding coffee spurted unceremoniously into the cardboard cup and the loose change clanged sonorously into the metal pocket below, she felt rejected and forlorn.

She had to stop thinking and there was only one thing that was going to make that happen; sitting at her workstation watching her favourite film on top-of-the-range equipment in lonely isolation.

She stared at the blank screen, blew on the bitter coffee, and slipped the DVD into the machine ready to press *Play*. Hannah knew what to expect: Credits displayed over a flat political map of Africa, a full western orchestra creating synthetic Arabic music conjuring up an image of timeless adventure and the mystery of the Kasbah, the melody melting into the Marseillaise and a revolving globe filling the screen setting the time with news of the relentless flow of refugees journeying to Casablanca.

She pressed *Play* but there were no credits, no map of Africa, no Marseillaise. Instead a still image of Humphrey Bogart appeared on the monitor. '*As Time Goes By*' filtered through the speakers and Rick uttered the unforgettable line, "Here's looking at you kid." There was a glitch and the still reappeared and the line was repeated. Another glitch, another still, the same line repeated over and over again.

"Here's looking at you kid."

"Here's looking at you kid."

"Here's looking at you kid."

Time goes by. Hannah presses the eject button – nothing

"Here's looking at you kid."

"Here's looking at you kid."

"Here's looking at you kid."

She presses the *eject* button a second time – nothing - hot coffee is spilt. Her skin is burning, and she wipes her hands on her jeans and presses the *eject* button again – press, press, and press, again and again.

"Here's looking at you kid."

"Here's looking at you kid."

"Look, look, looking, look after the kid. Look."

The frame flickers the image of Bogart disappears. The camera is on Ingrid Bergman, she is Elsa and she's beautiful. But she is fading, and another woman comes into shot; full *Technicolo*r fills the screen for another scene, another film. The woman wears Elsa's tears. She leans down and picks up a tapestry bag turns towards a familiar door. Colour fades and Elsa walks towards the plane.

Hannah wants to follow but she is burning. She is lost. Something is wrong.

Something is wrong.

"Is something wrong?" Hannah turns and sees a familiar figure in the doorway.

She wants to speak. It's a young woman, Jill no Jen. She'd worked alongside her when she first arrived. Jen was calm. She was nice.

She's speaking again.

"Can I help?"

Jen leaned over Hannah's shoulder and pressed the *eject* button. The screen went blank and the only sound to be heard was a faint whir as the DVD slid out of the player.

"But I did that…Nothing happened."

"Always the way, you press *Play* ten times and nothing happens then the tea lady comes along, does the very same thing and, hey presto, everything is working."

"It was so weird…I've never seen…heard anything like it…I mean it was no ordinary glitch."

"Must be gremlins! Want another coffee? We could go to the café around the corner."

"Thanks, but no thanks, I'm not exactly in a fit state to be seen in public."

"You'll be fine. The place is full of odd-bods and techie weirdoes." Adding quickly "They were right about the ending though. It probably was for the best."

"Sorry! What did you say?"

"It was probably for the best, you know, the end of the film. That's what my Nan always said anyway. What do you think?"

"I think" said Hannah, putting the DVD to one side, "I think coffee in a café full of odd-bods and techie weirdoes would probably be for the best."

Miriam

Miriam had been standing in the doorway of Blake's Rare and Antique Book Shop for nearly twenty minutes before it dawned on her that, maybe, she had got the wrong time. She knew for sure that she was in the right place because the whole reason for meeting up with her friend was so they could collect the books together before having a spot of lunch in the little café on the corner. And it had to be the right day because it would be the first time they would meet on a Saturday since their friendship began three months earlier. As the rain eased slightly she made a dash for the café thinking, perhaps, Bill would be there waiting for her and if he wasn't she could, at least, take the weight off her feet and consider what to do next.

Miriam found an empty seat by the window where she had a good view of Blake's book shop. It was also a perfect place to watch the comings and goings in the world outside. Despite the inclement weather, the little Market town was always busy on a Saturday morning. There was a tall, spindly, white haired gentleman in a morning suit wrestling with his umbrella and a young mother, upright and vigilant, facing the rain as she navigated a baby buggy that resembled a miniature, plastic greenhouse through the steady stream of sodden shoppers, who were all 'eyes down' heading for shelter and dodging in and out of doorways without due warning.

While she waited for her steaming, hot chocolate to cool Miriam checked her phone for messages but there was only one from the phone company which she deleted without reading. She was disappointed but not surprised to find that there was nothing from Bill. There were only two public phone boxes left in the town and they were often out of order. Miriam smiled to herself as she thought about Bill's almost evangelical dislike of mobile phones, smart or otherwise and anything to do with social media he found beyond the pale. Miriam, on the other hand, especially after her husband had died, would spend at least half-an-hour most evenings reading and writing emails and scrolling down her Facebook page, laughing, grimacing, and sometimes shouting at the screen in front of her. Computers and the Internet would be forever, something on which she and Bill would never agree. But it didn't matter they had so much else in common; their interest in old films, rare books, and black-and-white photographs for a start. But above all it was their love of poetry that had drawn them together.

Miriam had been sitting on a park bench, her tatty copy of 'The Collective Poems of William Wordsworth' resting on her lap. She had been unaware of the gentleman sitting next to her until, without warning, he said, "I wandered lonely as a cloud…" and, without thinking, she had replied, "…that floats on high o'er vales and hills." and laughing, they completed the first verse of the poem in unison.

From that day on they had spent many lunchtimes together, either sitting in the park eating their sandwiches or in the corner café where they would share a pot of tea and talk of many things: "Of shoes and ships and sealing-wax: Of cabbages and kings."

Occasionally, if time permitted before returning to work, they would visit Blake's Rare and Antique Book Shop, browsing the shelves and wondering how much longer Old Mr Blake would be able to keep trading. From the floor to the ceiling there were hundreds of carefully, lovingly catalogued books, old books. But there was little call for the several volumes of 'Encyclopaedia Britannica' that filled the stack at the rear end of the shop or the tiny 'Pitman's Pocket Shorthand Dictionary' nestled between a

'Brewers Dictionary of Phrase and Fable' and a 'Webster's New World Roget's A-Z Thesaurus'.

Yes, there were plenty of old books but as for rare ones they were, indeed, very rare. Miriam had been a good customer over the years and she knew that when Mr Blake said, "You keep this shop going," it wasn't far from the truth.

With the thought of Mr Blake and the excitement of picking up her new books, Miriam gulped down the last of the still quite hot chocolate, paid the bill and hurriedly made her way back to the book shop.

It had been just over two weeks ago when Mr Blake had told Miriam that he could get hold of the William Wordsworth's first edition. Published by London in 1807 the poems were in two volumes with contemporary binding and one of only 500 copies printed. Miriam had hesitated when he had told her the price but as Bill had pointed out it was an investment.

But Miriam knew that once the books were hers she would never part with them, so without further ado she had written out a cheque for £5,750 in the knowledge that she was purchasing a treasure and Blake's Rare and Antique Book Shop would trade another day.

When the bell rang out over the door, Old Mr Blake, with considerable difficulty, rose from his chair and slowly shuffled out from the back room where he spent most of his time surfing the web for rare books and then purchasing trunk loads of 'job lot' paperbacks. By the time he reached the counter Miriam was already sifting through the bargain box. She had her back to Mr Blake, but he knew who it was straight away. At least he thought he did.

"Miriam, is that you Miriam?"

Miriam turned; her smile swept away by the troubled look on the old man's face.

"Are you okay Mr Blake? Is there anything I can do?"

"No, no, I'm quite alright, but you my dear, you're not ill? Your friend, he was here, said you were ill, in hospital. I um, I wouldn't have, if I'd known, I wouldn't have…

Old Mr. Blake didn't need to say another word. Miriam already knew. Suddenly she was feeling unwell. She perched her bottom on the edge of the bargain box, in order to steady herself and take in what she knew to be true. She had been right about the time and she had been right about place. But, it seemed, to her cost, she had been woefully wrong about Bill.

Peculiar Pair

The Reverend Josephine Jennings had been looking forward to a day pottering about in the garden. Nothing too drastic; the small patch of grass required mowing and the Jack-by-the-Hedge needed pulling up before it blocked out all light from the front room window. Other than that she envisaged a great deal of sitting in the sun, drinking cups of tea and finishing 'Murder at The Vicarage' prior to returning it to the library first thing Monday morning, therefore avoiding a fine and a raised eyebrow from the ancient librarian who always gave her a 'vicars should know better' look.

But the phone call had put an end to her weekend plans, and she could only hope that the new assistant librarian with the dangly earrings would be on duty to help her use the scanning machine when she returned her book which would now most certainly be overdue. Oh, how she disliked those machines. The self-service checkouts in the supermarket were the same; no matter how hard she tried she inevitably ended up having to ask for help. Vegetables were a particular problem!

But what was she thinking? She had a wedding in less than an hour and the last thing the bride and groom needed after being informed that their own familiar vicar had been rushed to hospital with suspected appendicitis was a substitute priest more concerned with the complexities of scanning carrots rather than the holy sacrament that was about to take place on their wedding day.

So with a quick prayer and a change out of her gardening gear she arrived at the church with marriage on her mind.

Now, Josephine had seen some strange sights in her time but today she thought Mary and Jack, the couple standing in front of her 'took' as they say 'the biscuit' and judging by the size of the bride one too many biscuits had indeed been taken. As for the groom he was as skinny as his wife was fat. And what was even more astonishing their guests were also defined by their size. The groom's friends and relations seated on the right-hand side of the aisle were without exception extremely thin whereas the bride's family, quite definitely, were not.

And as for their clothes, The Reverend Josephine Jennings conceded God's own rainbow could not compare with the colour shimmering forth from the pews where the Mary's friends and family sat with their eyes fixed on the blushing bride: dresses and skirts, trousers and shirts in violet, purple and pink, ruby red, emerald green, and sapphire blue; spots and stripes, tie-dye and tartan, golden ribbons and silver lace trim.

As for Jack's side, the vicar had seen more colour in an undertaker's parlour; like keys on a piano they stood straight and thin as glimpses of white peered through black suits and cashmere overcoats.

However, as the young couple stood ready to make their vows Josephine saw beyond shape and size, colour, and cloth.

It was true Mary's floppy straw hat adorned with silk sweet peas exaggerated her round pink cheeks but the smile on that chubby face made her in Josephine's opinion the most beautiful bride she had ever seen. And as Jack, lean in his 'mourning' suit and black tie looked at his wife 'to be' with such undying love he was at that moment the most handsome of all men.

So when the oaths were made and rings exchanged The Reverend Josephine Jennings thought how glad she was to have been taken away from her book and cups of tea for, she believed, as they left the church for their reception at The Lamb and Lettuce, Mr and Mrs Jack Sprat would surely live happily ever after and lick their platters clean.

Meg

Meg was feeling utterly miserable and extremely tired. In a minute she would get up and try to make her living room live again but first she needed to rest, shut her eyes to the mess, press pause and try her best not to think. But that was the problem she simply couldn't stop thinking. How could she have been so stupid to get the wrong day. After weeks of waiting for a quotation, unanswered emails, countless, pointless phone calls, broken promises and the infernal, relentless drip, drip dripping keeping her awake night after night it was no wonder that she was feeling so fraught..

Her eyes opened with a jolt and she glanced at the calendar again: Thursday the 20th *'roofer 9.30'*. Why had she thought today was Wednesday? What had happened to Wednesday? She winced as she recalled the haughty, measured note in Donna's voice on the other end of the phone: "But it's Thursday today Mrs Buckingham. Our representative will be with you in thirty minutes, that's half an hour. Have you got that?" And in a blatantly unhelpful tone had added, "Is there anything else I can help you with?" If Meg could have looked into the future she would have replied: "Yes there is something you can bloody well do. You can dial 999 and call an ambulance because your representative, who happens to be called Ken by the way, is lying face down on my living room carpet and is in need of immediate medical attention. Have you got that?" But she wasn't a soothsayer and had called the emergency services herself, provided as many details as her panic-stricken brain could muster and prayed to some God or other that help would arrive in time.

It was no good she couldn't rest. She heaved herself out of the chair, collected up the cups and made her way into the kitchen. She had been silly to get into a state earlier, but she was still cross with herself for getting the dates mixed up. If she hadn't phoned she could have been spared the humiliation, the embarrassment of hearing the disdain in Donna's voice as she enunciated 'thirty minutes, that's half an hour." Meg took some comfort in the knowledge that even Miss Perfect could make mistakes. For one thing Donna had been wrong about the time of arrival, for no sooner had Meg put the phone down than a van proclaiming 'KKRoofing *No Job too big or too small!*'

pulled up outside the house and Ken was knocking on the door.

Meg had liked Ken straight away, something about him reminded her of Bill and despite her intention to remain cool she had found herself blithering about wrong days, sleepless nights and things being a bit untidy. With an easy smile he had said, "Not a problem. I'll just pop around the back and see what's what?" And once he had discovered what was what she had made a pot of tea while he reassured her that it was just a matter of replacing a few slate tiles. "A roof ladder will do. No need for scaffolding. My lad will fix it in a jiffy," he had explained.

No need for scaffolding, a roof ladder would do; Meg could have wept for joy. That was something else Mrs Donna, Hoity-toity, High-and-Mighty had been wrong about. She had been quite insistent that scaffolding would be essential, leaving Meg to wonder where on earth the money was going to come from. But work completed in a jiffy didn't sound too expensive, a bit more than the price of a lemon but still affordable. Meg was also pleased to hear the words 'my lad will fix it' because in all honesty she hadn't been able to imagine a ladder strong enough to hold Ken's excessive weight. It had been his unflappability and effortless kindness that had reminded her of her husband Bill but that was where the likeness came to an end. Ken was younger for a start, mid-forties maybe and unlike Bill he was very, very fat.

Of course Bill had put on a bit of weight after he had given up smoking, but everyone thought he looked better for it.

Meg twisted her wedding ring easily around her finger and thought of Bill. If only he had been with her then everything would be all right; he would be making his special scrambled eggs for lunch, the roof would be fixed, and who knows the sun might be shining.

But he wasn't there and there was washing up to be done. She rinsed out her cup and turned it upside down on the draining board to dry. She reached out for other one - the pale green one - raised it to her lips and remembered the smell of tea and flapjack and wood smoke and the large kind man sitting somewhat awkwardly on the tiny triangular campaign stool. She could see him clearly. He was rubbing his hands together and warming himself by the fire. He turned gracefully for a man of his size and held out his hand. It was only then that she had noticed the ID badge: Kenneth Kerani. She handed him his tea. "Here you are Mr Kerani. Would you like some flapjack, I made it myself?"

"It's Ken - yes please." He had liked her tea, appreciating the steeped taste of fresh leaves. He had admired her room and asked about the photographs and paintings that covered the once brilliant white walls, and for a moment Meg allowed herself to think that he had liked her too.

And then it was time for him to leave.

He had stretched out his hand to give her the cup but before she could take it from him he'd clasped it to his chest, his fingers clutching the tiny handle as if it were a talisman that would somehow keep him upright. But then, with an alarming howl, he fell to his knees. All the while he was holding the cup until, as if in surrender, he placed it carefully on the stool and slowly slipped face down onto the floor.

She had done all she could have done so why did she feel so wretched, so inept. She had managed with fumbling fingers to press the three numbers into her phone but failed to answer questions of breathing and pulse. She had successfully rolled the great bulk over onto his back but not without first knocking his head on the leg of the table. She had managed to undo the poppers on his padded jacket but then couldn't remember how many pumps and how many breaths should be applied.

But she had pumped and pumped and filled his lungs with her own breath until aching and weary she had slumped against the wall drifting into despondently at her own inadequacy. And in a moment of dog-tired delirium had contemplated hoovering around the body before the paramedics arrived. She had sat there imagining the rasping drone of the vacuum cleaner penetrating Ken's ear drum as he made ready to pay the ferry man and then, when eventually lifted onto the stretcher, there would be his vast form in the dust like a corpse outlined in chalk from a crime scene. *"Margaret Buckingham you have been found guilty of losing Wednesday and participating in over-zealous housework".*

A sudden painful picture of Bill lying alone on the cold muddy path with no one there to help had forced her on hands and knees back to Ken's side.

Meg had no memory of the ambulance arriving but could clearly see Judy's golden pony tail swaying against her emerald green uniform as she swung into action and there was the chatty one, the man, who had asked her questions she couldn't answer - and then they were gone. They were gone and she had done her best.

Meg realised that she was still holding the cup to her lips; carefully she dipped it into the soapy water; maybe, just maybe, it might be a lucky charm after all.

She really had to stop thinking such nonsense and rest. Her wrists tingled, her arms and shoulders throbbed, the pain in her back was intense and her neck was stiff; she ached all over. With energy almost spent she filled a hot water bottle and returned to her living room; she sank into the softly cushioned sofa and with feet up and the hot water bottle positioned at the base of her spine and she fell into a sumptuous sleep.

She woke abruptly to the sound of someone banging on the front door. Bewildered between sleep and wakefulness she eased her cold aching body off the sofa and made her way into the hall running her fingers through her hair in a feeble attempt to look more 'with it' before opening the door where she came face to face with a chubby young man with a nervous smile. He looked familiar but he was speaking so quickly it was all she could to follow what he was saying. "Mum sent me. I'm sorry I banged on the door, I did ring the bell, but you didn't answer, and mum said you'd be sure to be at home, so I banged on the door , sorry!"

Her mouth dry from sleep and her mind numbed by weariness Meg was ready to believe that the figure in front of her was nothing more than a figment of her imagination so she fixed her eyes on the young man's smile and waited to see if he would simply disappear. Her vacant stare did nothing to reassure the young man who was already shuffling from foot to foot and desperately trying to hold on to his wavering smile. But he didn't waver and pointing to a van that Meg had not noticed parked by the gate went on to explain that he had come to fix the roof.

"Mum told me to come round and fix it and say thanks for all you did for dad; they reckon he's going to be alright. Mum says it's all thanks to you, so she sent me around to um – I'll come back later if you want."

Ever so slowly Meg was beginning to make sense of things. This was Ken's lad and Ken was going to be alright. "No please, please don't go, please stay. I'm sorry; I'm just a little tired you know. But please don't go."

An easy smile stretched across the young man's face.

"Right, okay," he said, "I'll just go and get m' ladder. Mum will give me a right earful if I don't get it done this afternoon."

Something told Meg that she knew the answer to the next question, but she needed to ask anyway, "Do I know your mother?"

Later, lying in bed listening to the rain pelting against the window Meg was trying to ignore the jumble of random thoughts and unanswered questions that were keeping her awake. Was Ken still in intensive care? Was Donna giving him 'an earful' too? Was Donna the same Donna who had been so unpleasant in the morning the same Donna who had insisted on the roof being fixed free of charge? No need for a ladder - fixed in a jiffy - no time for tea. No time for flapjack. Was it the Flapjack Ken? Flap jack, camels back, heart attack; green cups and talismans, purple bumps, and a golden pony tail, faded white walls and a Wednesday lost, a lad with a ladder, Ken's lad, kind Ken, Ken like Bill, no more Bill. No more drip, drip ,drip dripping , no more drip, drip, dripping no more drip, dripping.

Fen Meadow

As Stephanie opened the bedroom window and looked through her binoculars out across the flat landscape she felt something near to happiness. She could make out the purple moor-grass pushing its way through the reeds and bottle sedge, and there between the sharp flowered rush, creamy white and softly flowering, meadowsweet; its almond fragrance seeping into the dank odour of marsh and mud. She could see the straight narrow road they had towed the caravan along earlier, and the lay-by where they had stopped to watch the sun rise, and there was the gate they had climbed to get a better view of the house.

"There it is." she had said, "Fen Meadow."

Seeing the house for the first time in over thirty years Stephanie thought it looked lost as if somehow it had been inexplicably dropped on to the black earth by mistake. There again she had thought the letter from Stidwell, Garland and Frost had been a mistake. But there had been no error and after a great deal of jumping through legal hoops Stephanie found herself sole beneficiary of her late Great Uncle Percy's estate. And part of Great Uncle's estate was Fen Meadow, a rambling, ramshackle, biscuit brick, and slate roof house in need of tender loving care.

She put the binoculars down on the window sill, her thoughts interrupted by Leonard calling up the stairs.

"Steph old girl, come and have a look at this."

Steph? Old girl? How and when did that happen, and more to the point why didn't it bother her? Not so long ago she would have given short shrift to anyone for saying such a thing. But now she simply walked over to the door and shouted back

"Just a minute."

She wanted to stay a while longer in the room where she had slept during the warm summer months all those years ago and perhaps catch the haunting call of the snipe or the curlew's mournful cry echoing across the fens. But all was silent; empty and silent. The room was bare, save for a few faded shreds of cream and gold damask wallpaper that she had started to strip away from the surprisingly dry walls. All the rooms were the same, empty! There were no curtains, carpets, or light bulbs anywhere to be seen. Except, that is, in the surgery below.

When Great Uncle Percy had locked the front door thirty years earlier he had taken everything with him. Later, when they were drinking tea in his new flat, Stephanie had asked him why; he simply said,

"Needed most of it - anyway thought the place was in need of a new broom."

If Stephanie had known then that it would be her doing the sweeping, she would have questioned him further about the surgery and why he had left everything intact.

"Don't need any of it; doctoring days are over." was all he had said.

Oh, and with a wink and a furtive smile he had slipped in, "Maybe you're not the only one with a skeleton in their cupboard."

The happiness Stephanie had felt earlier was now replaced by a familiar melancholy as once again her mind was swamped with the one memory she longed to forget. If her great uncle had been trying to make her feel better that day over tea and biscuits it had worked for while. For days after she had imagined all sorts of scandals, indiscretions, or even criminal activities that the distinguished Percival Browning MD might have committed. But it wasn't long before guilt returned with anger in tow. 'Guilt and Anger' - guilt for what she had done and anger because the one person she had most wanted to support and comfort her had told her to stop behaving like a prima Donna and 'get on with it'! Stephanie hadn't been able to get on with it and when eventually she handed in her notice putting an end to a regular pay packet coming into the house her not so supportive husband upped and left her for someone, who in Stephanie's opinion really was a prima Donna.

Over the years guilt and anger had merged into a manageable melancholy. She retrained as a radiographer and returned to work. On good days she caught herself laughing at a shared joke with colleagues and friends. And then of course there was Leonard. Leonard who had been so enthusiastic about selling his cottage and restoring an old fenland house into a home they could both be happy in. Stephanie wanted to happy. The question was, could she be?

"Well you won't know until you try," Great Uncle Percy would have said and with that in mind she closed the window and went down the back stairs that led directly into the old waiting room.

Stephanie could still picture, what to her young eyes had seemed, ancient creatures staring blankly at the 'Coughs and Sneezes Spread Diseases' poster on the wall or flicking through the pages of out of date 'Woman's Owns'. She remembered her Great Uncle saying that many of his patients, despite their aches and pains, had to walk the one and half miles from the village to get a prescription to relieve them of the inevitable lumbago and arthritis that was part and parcel of living on damp fenlands and a lifetime of backbreaking work. She could hear him say "Lot's to be grateful for my dear," and with that thought she entered, what she had come to believe was, the slightly suspect surgery.

"Ah, there you are have a look at this."

Leonard was holding a wooden frame with a handle on the central rod.

"Must've been used for winding something up."

"Bandages, it's a bandage winder," she said.

"Ah yes, now what about this?" Placing the frame carefully back on the shelf Leonard led her over to the other side of the room where there was a wooden box lined with metal trays and containing a bow saw and three all metal, ridged, graded knives. "Says here it was made by Down Bros of St Thomas' Street, 1910, what d'you reckon?"

Stephanie peered into the box and knew straight away.

"It's an amputation set, belonged to my great grandfather. He served in the Royal Army Medical Corps during World War 1. Most of the stuff in here belonged to him. Great Uncle Percy couldn't bear to get rid of it."

"Quite right too, this place is an absolute museum." Leonard's enthusiasm was contagious, and Stephanie took pleasure in explaining how a hip joint drill or tonsil guillotine would have worked and just when she thought he might be getting bored he would ask another question.

"And what about this, do you know what's in here?" He pulled the privacy screen to one side to reveal a large metal cabinet in the corner of the room. Stephanie had never set eyes on the cabinet in her life but the very fact that it was there, occupying the space where the wooden hat and coat stand should be positioned next the treatment couch, brought about a rush of anxiety which was only curbed by a greater sense of curiosity.

Leonard was saying something about finding a key in the desk drawer. "It looks as if should fit do you want to do the honours?"

Stephanie took the key and slipped it into the lock. There was a rasp of metal on metal as the key turned. The door swung open and there lynched on the misplaced hat and coat stand was a human skeleton.

Stephanie's eyes were fixed on the hardened plastic bones before her and without any warning words that had wormed their way into the pit of her very being were about to be unleashed. "Leonard I need to tell you something."

"Oh, okay, old girl but let's go out into the sunshine shall we and I'll get you a cup of tea."

They sat side by side on the cast iron bench and sipped the slightly fusty tasting tea that comes from being in a thermos too long.

"Leave your personal life behind at the hospital door and focus entirely on the patients in your care. It was a golden rule," Stephanie said.

"I broke the rule. We'd had a row over money, and I couldn't get the hurtful remarks out of my head. There was an elderly gentleman in bay four who had suffered a severe stroke and he kept pressing the call bell. He was confused and wanted to go home. I reassured him that he was in safe hands. He would drift back to sleep, and I would drift back to the ugly row. It hadn't been a particularly busy night, maybe that's why I was distracted. Anyway, I was making ready for the early morning medication round when he pressed the call button again. This time I didn't try to get him back to sleep but raised the back of the bed, plumped up his pillows and told him I'd be back in a little while with his medication. One of the young orderlies had just brought me a cup coffee when we heard the crash and the startled cry. And I knew then, even before we had reached the bay; I knew I'd forgotten pull up the cot rail." Stephanie sipped her tea, but it was hard to swallow.

"There was no disciplinary action and the family couldn't have been kinder. But he died Leonard. He died because of me; he died because he wasn't in safe hands."

Leonard put his arm around her.

It only took a gentle touch and Stephanie wept decades of tears. The melancholy that had been so much a part of her for so many years was being washed away. Sorrow was spent in the morning sun and in the distance breaking the silence they could just make out the cry of a Curlew.

"Not a cheery chap is he?" said Leonard.

Stephanie smiled, "Wait till you here the snipe. Thank you for listening."

"I'm glad you told me. How are you feeling now?"

"Better." She was feeling better and it was the cue Leonard needed to start 'getting on' with things.

"So, shall we go and let our bony companion out of his cupboard? We could open up a museum and Fred, he looks like a Fred, I knew a particularly skinny corporal once called Fred. He could meet visitors at the door. What d'you think?"

"Well, I think Great Uncle Percy would be delighted but our receptionist will have to be Freda not Fred!"

"Crikey," Said Leonard "If I'd known, I would have averted my eyes."

Stephanie laughed. Leonard's archaic vocabulary certainly belonged in a museum. Maybe opening up the surgery to the public really wasn't such a bad idea after all. But first, there was work to be done if the house was going to be their home.

"Right then, for modesty's sake, I'll let Freda out and then carry on upstairs."

"Okay, I'll pop into the village. That little hardware shop should be open by now. I'll get a new gas bottle so we can make a decent cup of tea. Anything you want?"

"There's something but it's slipped my mind, can't be that important." And just as Leonard was about to get in the car it came to her and she shouted after him. "I've remembered what it was."

"What's that old girl?"

"A broom; we need a new broom."

The Summer Fair

For five days the otherwise ordinary little town burst into hedonistic revelry: Music, dancing, cream teas, a sticky bun race, fancy dress, and Tug of War. Len loved it all. But best of all there were five whole drinking days when Dot let him be.

It was Saturday night and with a pint of Otter close to his chest Len stared with pride at the red white and blue bunting that hung from the Town Hall. He belonged. What more could a man want other than a good wife, friends and a full glass in his hand.

He looked over at the children in fancy dress queuing for hotdogs and was pleased to see that pirates and princesses were still old favourites. He saw Molly give Dot a hug and thought she looked a picture. What had she said earlier?

"Don't be silly Granddad, I'm not Tinkerbelle, I'm Princess Elsa."

He had put his hand in his pocket and fumbled to find some change but when he looked up Molly had disappeared behind the group of freshly scrubbed farmers standing around the cider barrels.

Len watched as Alfie Buckland, who still in his drum majorette costume hurled a bale of hay on to the trailer and makeshift stage. It took two pale, raven haired lads to drag the hay bale behind the drum kit, complaining all the while about not being the frigging Wurzles. "It's that or the Fare Queen's throne" barked Alfie. The boys didn't argue.

"Lovely legs Alf"…said Len. "What are you having?"

"Cheers mate…a pint of Sam's"

Len emptied his glass and as he turned he thought he saw the back of Bert Saunders walking towards the church. He made a note to catch up with him later and buy him a drink. He was glad that Bert was out and about again. Len stood for a moment looking at Dot. She looked up and smiled at him. Life was perfect and just for a moment Len thought he might cry.

* * * * *

Bert Saunders's daughter had said it would do him good to get out. She was right the walk had raised his spirits. Avenues of beech cast a welcome shade as he made the three-mile trek to town. He had seen a pair of Pied Wagtails, a Bullfinch, a Meadow Pipette, and had followed a family of partridges from Leigh Cross to Tanner's farm where dozens of House Martins had feasted on flies from the chicken shed. But on reaching town Bert wished he was home again. He felt as washed out as the faded bunting that hung out over the Town Hall. It was Mai who loved the Summer Fair. She loved it all, the dog show, apple bobbing, the flower festival and after a few barley wines dancing in the street. It wasn't the same without her.

Dot Turner caught his eye. She beckoned him over and handed him a steaming hotdog.

"On the house Bert…How are you keeping?"

"Not so bad - yourself?"

"Can't complain"

"Len Here?"

"Since lunch time…want another?"

The long walk had given him an appetite.

"Well if they're going spare don't mind if I do."

A line of children were waiting to be served so with a nod and a "thanks" he crossed the road and sat on the bench outside side the newsagents and ate the second hotdog. He watched a girl in some kind of fairy dress hugging Dot, it had to be little Molly. She was the image of her grandmother; the girl he remembered from junior school.

He could see the playground as if it were yesterday. They were lined up for the fancy-dress parade, boys on one side girls on the other. Lindy Gibb was Red-Riding-Hood, and her sister Nell was Cinderella, Mai was Snow White and Dot Tinkerbelle. He was Captain Hook, Len was Long-John-Silver and little Alfie Buckland Jim Hawkins. Then there was sad Elsie Judd who they all said was one of the ugly sisters and poor Davy Miller who went as himself, but Miss Walker had given him a bowl and put a sign around his neck saying, 'Oliver Twist' and he'd won first prize.

The 'not so little' Alfie Buckland walked passed carrying a bale of hay on his shoulder. How Mai would have laughed at those great hairy legs and hobnail boots. Bert watched the pink wig fall to the ground as Alfie tossed the bale of hay onto the make shift stage and if it were no more than a handful of feathers. It was then that he heard a familiar voice:

"Lovely legs Alf"… "What are you having?"

It was Len talking. Bert got up and walked towards the churchyard. He wanted to talk to Mai. He would catch up with Len later.

Stalemate

Harry and Ted had been friends since primary school. They had been drawn together by their mutual dislike of sport and became firm friends, when in their final year, before going to the big school, they signed up for Mr. Johnson's a lunchtime chess club. After two terms the boys were expert at the game and both managed to beat Mr. Johnson on more than one occasion. Early in the third term Mr. Johnson decided to give up the chess club and concentrate instead on 'passing and dribbling skills' with the under-sevens football team. Harry and Ted tried to keep the club going but numbers soon dwindled and before long it was just the two of them and a couple of girls from their class. Rosemary Brooks played a decent game but her friend Miranda Drew wasn't that interested, preferring instead to have her nose stuck in a book. But, as the boys soon discovered, Miranda could make unexpected moves and they had to keep their wits about them.

The two boys remained friends during their five years at the newly built Comprehensive School and Community College. However, as time passed they saw less of one another. Harry, determined to go to university to read Law, spent a considerable amount of his spare time studying, while Ted was frequently absent from school helping out on the family farm. His non-attendance was particularly noticeable during lambing time and silage making.

At eighteen, Harry was offered a place at Swansea University, not however to read law, but on the advice of Mr Cricklewood, his careers teacher, to study Mathematics. With a BSc tucked under his belt he secured a job at a minor public school and within three years he was head of department, a position he held until taking early retirement due to a painful stomach ulcer. A condition brought on by having to keep up with the constantly changing teaching methods inflicted on schools across the country by so called specialists, who, in Harry's mind, wouldn't survive five minutes in a class of thirty adolescent boys.

Therefore, with a bottle of single malt whiskey, a farewell present from the staff, a small suitcase and a trunk full of books he returned to his childhood home.

When Harry's mother had died he had let out Ivy Cottage to a young professional couple who were waiting to get a foot on the housing ladder. Retirement meant having to give the couple three months notice to leave.

They had taken good care of the furnished cottage so there was nothing for Harry to do other than move his few processions into his old home and make contact with his oldest friend. Christmas and birthday cards had been exchanged but they hadn't met since Harry was best man at Ted's wedding. Harry had no desire to marry, indeed he had no particular interest in women, but he did concede that Ted, was indeed, very fortunate to have won the heart of Miranda Drew.

It was as if he had never been away. The two men talked with ease and it wasn't before long, that it became something of a ritual, to meet one evening a week in the back room of the Black Horse for a pint or two of Gold Tap and a game of chess.

They never tired of each others company. They never tired of chess. There was never any rancour in defeat. Equally matched, they accepted that both were capable of making careless moves and always, without hesitation, acknowledged who had played the better game. If, on the rare occasion, stalemate was inevitable, the one who had played the weaker game would knock over their king and buy the next round.

Tuesdays was their chosen night. It was generally quiet. Friday was darts night and even in the little room, with the open fire in the winter, they could hear the raucous shouts coming from the public bar. It was just as bad on the third Thursday of the month when there was a quiz. They were a noisy bunch too. Harry was aware that they raised money for different charities, but he hated them all the same and made sure not to pop into the Black Horse for a quick half when they were taking place. Hence, his heart sank, when one morning in September, Miranda turned up on his doorstep, bearing a pot of homemade blackberry jam and asked if, because of a sad and unexpected death, he would make up numbers on a team for the next quiz. It was, she told him, to raise money for cancer research, a charity Harry knew was close to her heart.

Harry couldn't say no.

He barely knew his three team mates. Dorothy and Jack Huggins lived just around the corner from Ivy cottage, but they hardly ever saw each other, let alone made conversation. He'd met the tall, spectacled gentleman in the bright orange fleece a couple of times while queuing in the post office and they had passed the time of day but he didn't know his name which was something of an embarrassment, as his team mate, on more than one occasion had said, "One for you Harry, I bet you know the answer to this".

Harry had answered a few questions, but they were generally, the ones that the rest of the team also knew. He felt as if, he may as well of not been there, that is until, nearing the end of the second half, when Ted, the quiz master for the evening asked, "In Greek mythology, how did Icarus meet his fate?" Jack Huggins was quick to whisper, "His wings melted" and with the other two in agreement started writing the answer on the sheet of paper in front of him. Leaning forward so as not be heard, Harry pointed out that, if they were establishing how Icarus died, it was in fact by drowning. He didn't deny that his wings had melted when he flew too near to the sun, but, Icarus fell into the sea and was therefore drowned. The team was now divided. The man in the orange fleece agreed with Harry while Dorothy and Jack, believed that in pub quiz tradition, the more commonly known fact about Icarus's demise would be what Jack had said in the first place. It was only when Ted went on to the next question that Jack hurriedly wrote down 'drowning'.

When the answer to that particular question was read out, Ted was adamant, the answer on sheet in front of him was the only one he'd accept, and it said, quite clearly, that Icarus met his fate when he flew too near the sun and his wings melted. Harry tried to argue his case but was stopped in his tracks when Ted made a wisecrack about looking it up on the coroner's report and ripples of laughter went around the public bar. Embarrassed and humiliated Harry made his way home as soon as the final results had been announced. They had come third, which according to Dorothy was their best result ever and that she hoped Harry would join them again the following month. He had feigned a smile and told her that he would see. What he had wanted to say was that he would never set foot in the Black Horse again, not for a quiz, not for anything.

Once home he forewent his usual cup of cocoa, opened the previously untouched bottle of single malt, and downed two generous measures in a matter of seconds, in the hope of erasing the evening from his mind. But sleep did not come. Lying in bed with the liquor wheedling its way into every crevice of his mind, the humiliation and hurt Harry had felt was turning to anger. He didn't care about coming first or last in the quiz, but he did care about being humiliated, and by Ted of all people.

Why had Ted not said, "Sorry, Harry old chap, you're quite right but we always go for the answer on the card?" That way it would have been a sort of stalemate and Harry would have abided by the rules of the game and graciously accepted defeat. But no, Ted had dismissed Harry's answer outright and, worse still, he had mocked him. The clock ticked and Harry tossed and turned. He imagined Ted and Miranda walking home together, arm in arm, laughing at Harry's expense, 'tick-tock', he was nothing more than a figure of fun, 'tick-tock', a lonely soul to be humoured with a weekly game of chess. The clock ticked and time mocked. Years of self pity and regret spewed out into the dark and a cold, clammy resentment, for those who had betrayed him, slid under the covers and into his aching heart. Mr. Cricklewood, who hadn't listened when Harry said he wanted to study law. The Headmaster and every single member of staff at that bloody awful school; not one of them had noticed that he never drank whisky, not one of them had thought that perhaps giving it to someone with a stomach ulcer was not a good idea.

'Tick-tock', the clock mocked. 'Tick-tock', Ted had mocked. 'Tick-tock', anger rolled and rocked.

Revenge, Harry wanted revenge.

A cool calm descended. His breathing became shallow as he allowed his mind to settle on vendetta.

Sometime, shortly after half-past-one, while contemplating purchasing potassium cyanide Harry fell into a fitful sleep.

He was flying towards an orange ball of fire. Someone was shouting at him to turn back but Harry couldn't stop. Wretched souls with scorched faces and melting grins were beckoning him into the light. Charred fingers poked and pulled at his hair. He had to turn. He had to fall. Spinning, spiralling, falling ever downwards, he plunged into cool clear waters. A hand on the back of his neck held him down as the wave crashed over his naked body.

A tall, spectacled man in an orange jumpsuit, marching swiftly along the beach stopped to pull the body out of the water. "I told you to turn around, now look what you've done." He bent down and rolled the corpse onto his back. Harry looked down and saw the lifeless, butcher bone blue face of his old friend and a wept. "No time for blubbing" said the man in orange "You're going to have to defend yourself" and he handed Harry a clipboard and a barrister's wig before heading off down the beach.

As dawn was breaking Harry woke from his dream with a headache, a heavy heart and the sound of the telephone ringing downstairs. Half asleep and unsteady on his feet he made his way down the narrow stairs, trying all the while to remember his dream, but it was gone. The tiles on the kitchen floor were cold and he wished he'd stopped to put on his dressing gown and slippers. If it was a wrong number at this time in the morning he would be none too pleased.

But it wasn't the wrong number. It was Miranda.

Moving On

As Sarah stood by the window and watched the removal van lumbering up the potholed lane memories of what had taken place the previous Friday, were once again threading through her mind. How the day had begun was clear enough, as too was how it ended. Everything else was a jumble of jagged images: dusty wine bottles, empty glasses, rough hands, blood, and scissors in her hands. She needed to remember everything, so she could tell Dan when he finally arrived. After all it was his idea that they move in, to the middle of nowhere. To give our children a better place to grow up in is what he had said. Sarah wasn't certain that she wanted children, let alone know the best place to raise them. As a born and bred city girl she felt that easy access to libraries, museums, and art galleries, together with not having to drive miles to the nearest health club or supermarket, far outweighed fresh air and clotted cream. But Dan was a country boy and she had agreed to the move to please him. Now, as the removal van disappeared from sight, her old life before the snowstorm seemed not days, but years behind her.

On Friday morning everything had gone to plan. She had left at first light, leaving Dan to supervise loading the grandmother clock onto the removal van. With everything needed for making a cup of tea at the other end, she had pulled out of their drive for the last time and driven to Hansworth, to pick up their gardening tools from the sorry looking shed on the now abandoned allotment. From here she had phoned Dan who had told her that the removal men were just about to leave, and that with luck everything should be unloaded at the other end shortly after midday. He would follow the van and ring her once they had reached the village. With a promise to put the kettle on, Sarah left Birmingham behind and by eight thirty she was driving towards the Malvern Hills, with a snowy sky overhead.

Six hours later she was on an un-gritted lane less than a mile away from their new home. She was tired and there was no signal on her phone. The last time she had heard from Dan, he and the men in the removal van were parked up miles away in a service station. Gritters were out on the motorway but there was little or no chance of them clearing the B roads and the police had advised them to stay put.

Sarah had managed to reach the village, gingerly crawling along narrow lanes that were layered with packed snow, making it impossible to brake without skidding out of control.

She had seen the tractor coming in plenty of time and managed to pull tight into the hedge. A tall, thick set figure climbed down from the cab and walked over to the car. She pressed the door lock on the ignition and opened the window just far enough to be heard.

"Can you get past? I don't think I'll be able to reverse."

"Where're you going to? Not far in this, I should say," was the old man's reply as he thumped the roof of what Sarah now realised was a very flimsy Ford Fiesta that a man of his build could probably smash with his bare hands.

"Oh right. I'm trying to get to The Old Rectory, Oakwell Lane"

"Well, that is as maybe but you won't make it up the hill."

"If I walk will the car be alright here?"

The man looked about for an answer, that appeared to be hidden on the road below, and in the sky above, and when satisfied with his findings, he pulled at his cap. "You 'ang' on 'ere' for a minute while

I go and turn round. You can follow me back to our yard. Ivy will know what to do."

It took less than five minutes for him to edge past Sarah's car, and turn in an open field but time enough for Sarah to wish that she was parked up safely alongside Dan in a service station rather than being jammed against a hedge, in a blizzard, at the mercy of a complete stranger. She had been relieved to hear the mention of a woman's name and hoped upon hope that, whoever Ivy was, she would indeed know what to do, and help Sarah reach the Old Rectory before nightfall. But the snow was relentless and by the time the tractor had turned, the tiny Ford was well and truly stuck, and the only practical solution was to be towed up the steep hill to Oakwell Farm.

Sarah couldn't remember ever feeling so cold. It had only been a short walk across the yard to the back porch, but the snow had seeped through her Lee Cooper canvas boots, soaking her socks, and numbing her toes. The old man removed his boots and following his example she bent down to untie the sodden, tightly knotted laces.

She could feel the old man's eyes fixed on her fumbling fingers. "You go ahead." she said, "I'll follow when I've got these undone."

"Leave 'em' be. Ivy will know what to do."

And Ivy had known what to do and Sarah had soon found herself, sitting by a wood - burning stove, wearing an oversized, red and white, cable knit cardigan, that hung unceremoniously beyond the knees of her jogging pants and a pair of Ivy's pale blue, fluffy bed socks. She felt extremely un-cool but very warm. When the old man removed his hat, Sarah realised Tom, as was his name, was not such an old man at all, but probably no more than fifty. It was difficult to tell with his weather - beaten face and shortage of teeth. Ivy, she guessed, was a little younger. She was also one of the fattest women Sarah had ever set eyes on. But Ivy was kind which was just as well, because there was no way Sarah was going to reach the Old Rectory that evening, and she was genuinely thankful for Ivy's offer of a bed and something to eat.

"Got a piece of lamb in the oven; just need to do some veg."

When Sarah had apologised for being a vegetarian, Tom had stomped out of the kitchen mumbling something about "Vegetarian! Whatever next?" and slammed the door behind him.

"Don't mind him. You can eat the veggies this evening and tomorrow I'll make you nice a nut roast. What d'you say?"

Sarah didn't know what to say, she had planned on being in her own home the next day, but she managed a, "Lovely! Thank you very much!"

Tom's sisters', Olive and Edith, joined them for supper, and it was at this point in the evening that Sarah's memory of events was less than clear. She remembered Ivy saying that Olive and Edith lived in the converted barn across the yard, and that they were a formidable pair and it was best to steer clear of talking about politics and religion, as they tended to be rather uncompromising in their views.

They had, Sarah recollected, brought with them several bottles of home-made wine for tasting. The Elderflower was delicious, as was the Blackberry. The Gooseberry had a definite bite to it and the Parsnip wine had made Sarah's eyeballs go numb. She remembered one of the sisters saying something about having a woman for Pope. However, by the time they got to the pea wine she couldn't recall anything that was said, apart from the fact that whatever it was, it was very funny and in her mother's words she thought Olive and Edith were *good craic*.

The next thing she remembered was being in bed and dreaming. How strange she thought, while so much of that evening was a blur, she could recall her dream - and as she did, fragments of memory began to form into something close to a clear picture of what happened next.

She had been dreaming about trying to paint the inside of the allotment shed, but she kept putting down the brush and forgetting where it was. Just at the moment she thought she could remember, she became aware of rough hands, ice cold hands, shaking her shoulder and an unfamiliar voice demanding that she should get up. She had opened her eyes and immediately shut them against the blinding light, and the terrifying sight of a bare-chested man bending, leaning, leering over her; foul breath from a gaping mouth was closing in on her. The voice behind the spray of spit was frantic. "Wake up! Ivy's not right, for pity's sake wake up! Ivy's not herself."

Sarah opened her eyes for a second time and bore the light. Her mouth was dry, she was in Ivy and Tom's house and there was Tom, dressed only in his underwear standing over her. A scream from another room made her sit up abruptly. She was awake and sober and still wearing the cable knit cardigan, jogging pants and fluffy socks.

"You must be cold," she said.

"Never mind me; it's Ivy who's not right."

By the time they reached the bedroom, Ivy was soaked with sweat but her cries had subdued. She began reassuring Tom that she would be alright and calmly informed Sarah that she might need a bit of help. "Tom's delivered dozens of lambs but he's no good with babies."

Sarah was about to protest; that as a childless writer of cookery books, she knew far less about babies than Tom; but was stopped in her tracks by Ivy, having another contraction and releasing a sound so intense, so primeval, that Sarah found herself acting out a role from one or more of the films she had seen, where child birth, was a crucial part of the plot.

"Towels, Tom now - then get dressed and get help."

"I'm on me way. Don't you worry none, Ivy will know what to do."

Now, as she sat on the makeshift seat in her unpacked house, Sarah wondered if she really had delivered Ivy's baby or had it been some sort of pea wine hallucination? But no, she had done it. She had really done it. Luckily things had gone in her favour. For a start there was an old -fashioned sink in the corner of the room where she could scrub up, and the dress maker's scissors on the dressing table came in handy for cutting up sheets for swaddling. Then there was Tom who had made every effort to reach the village on the tractor but had to give up and spent the rest of the night, bringing cups of tea and words of encouragement. And, when it was all over, Sarah knew she would never forget Tom's gaping smile, as he held his baby daughter for the first time.

"I think we should call her Sarah," said Ivy

"Don't know about that," he had said. "Might turn her into a vegetarian!"

The Wine Taster

Andrew always fancied himself as a bit of a wine connoisseur much to the irritation of Fiona, his wife of ten years and mother of their two children, Donald seven and Isabella five. Fiona's idea of a good bottle wine was what was on offer in Tescos and that didn't leave her with a headache. But, Fiona wasn't Andrew and as already stated Andrew thought he knew a thing or two about wine, boasting that he could tell his Beaujolais from his Burgundy with a sniff and swish and spit, but not mentioning a quick peak at the label.

His colleagues at the bank, like Fiona, were as aggravated as they were bored when he harped on about his sensitive pallet when it came to the subtleties of fine wine tasting. It was therefore no surprise that they were shocked and amazed and a little humbled when he announced that he had been invited to a wine tasting convention in Los Angeles. Cashiers and bank manager alike had to admit that for Andrew, a junior bank clerk of some years, to be invited to such an event was indeed a great accolade.

On the morning of his flight to California, Fiona had with pride and a considerable amount of guilt for the disagreement they had had over breakfast that morning kissed him on the cheek and wished him a fond farewell and good luck with the prestigious event. Andrew did not consider it a question of luck but as a man of such good standing accepted his wife's wishes and headed off to Heathrow Airport. He was travelling light: wash bag, camera three shirts, three ties, sufficient underwear, best suit, black shoes, and a copy of Maurice de Rouen's Guide to the wines of the Loire Valley; all neatly packed, by no one other than himself, in his new John Lewis Tourist Bon Air wheelie suitcase.

With a certain amount of anxiety and a tremendous feeling of excitement he steered his way through the London streets eager to be on the M4 that would take him to the airport and miles away from work and family. His anxiety increased when he slowed down and came to a halt behind a stationary black taxi only to see a long row of cars at a standstill behind a double-decker bus that blocked any further view of the road. Not wanting to waste fuel he turned off the engine and hoped that it was traffic lights causing the delay ahead. He stopped tapping his fingers on the dashboard and wound down the window when he noticed the taxi driver getting out of his cab and making his way towards Andrew's car.

"Won't be long I trust?" He asked the taxi driver.

"Sorry mate, there's been an accident. Some clown on a motor bike knocked an old geezer over and then scarpered."

"That's terrible," sighed Andrew.

"Sure is – bloody maniac."

Andrew was actually thinking it was terrible because he might miss his flight. But being a gentleman he refrained from saying such a thing.

The taxi driver wandered down the road imparting his knowledge to the drivers behind Andrew. Twenty minutes passed before the traffic started to move but in Andrew's mind he had been tapping his fingers on the dashboard for days.

Every light was red; every pedestrian crossing was crossed by crocodiles of school children and old people with Zimmer frames. When stuck behind a cyclist for at least thirty seconds he was tempted to shout at him to bugger off to the country and not take up precious space on a busy London road. But he didn't swear he was after all a gentleman.

However, swear he did and vehemently so when he reached the car park he had purposely booked so as to be within walking distance of his terminal, only to discover a notice informing motorists that the area was temporary closed and all travellers should proceed to Longford, Car Park C where a shuttle ran every ten minutes to Terminal 3. The *'We are sorry for any inconvenience'* only aggravated Andrew's ill humour as did the two young women he found himself standing next to on the shuttle who, in Andrew's opinion, had more luggage than sense and had talked nonstop for the full ten minutes' drive.

There was, for a moment, slight relief when the check in, which is normally a long and tedious procedure, went relatively smoothly. The feeling was, however, short lived thanks to the young man at border control who, when he passed his hands over Andrew's rear end in a search for hidden weapons, had in Andrew's mind been altogether too enthusiastic.

Despite all plans to give himself plenty of time for a leisurely cup of coffee Andrew had to carry rather than wheel his new John Lewis suitcase and run to the departure lounge at full speed. By the time he reached the gate he was hot and bothered and ready for a fight.

Never before had he felt so uptight. Uptight that was what Fiona had called him. She had called him unreasonable and uptight over breakfast and had completely put him off his boiled egg. She knew that he disliked the underground and yet she had gone on and on about the tube being quicker than driving. And then there was the inevitable, innocuous 'Wouldn't be the end of the world' comment.

"Wouldn't be the end of the world, to sit next to strangers for once in your life! "

'Wouldn't be the end of the world now would it' was one of her favourite expressions and one he hated above all others. But he hadn't been uptight; simply frustrated that he hadn't had time to tell his silly wife how annoyed he was with her. Andrew was just considering what he would say to her on his return when the call to board the plane was announced.

The lift off was smooth and soon London was fading from sight. The dockside warehouses, the river and roads were now nothing more than a child's model plaything.

Although Andrew hadn't eaten anything since the night before the smell of braised steak and overcooked vegetables gave him no appetite at all. He took one bite of the sticky pink cake but in the end settled for drinking the complimentary bottle of wine - a simple merlot which was but not bad, not bad at all. So much so he had another and another and another.

A few more later he was pushing the steward away. "How dare you touch me? Don't you know who I am?"

The steward tried his best. "Please sir, can you please stop shouting. The rest of the passengers are trying to sleep."

"I'm not bloody shouting" said Andrew very loudly while taking a swing at the steward.

It took two stewards, a vicar, and an elderly woman wielding a hair brush to drag Andrew to the back of the plane where they strapped him on an emergency medical stretcher.

Andrew came to in the immigration office in LAX where officials were sorting out papers for his immediate return to the U.K. For the immigration Officers it was just another job, just another idiot they had to deal with. However, for Andrew, gentleman, and wine taster it was the end of the world.

Vera

When Vera thought about bumping off her ex-husband it wasn't revenge that came to mind it was justice. For over a quarter of a centenary she had put up with his rabid temper and punishing fist. He had stolen those years from her and now he was basking in the sun with a woman half his age, spending what was left of their savings on Pina Coladas and Amber Solaire. There was no question in Vera's mind that William John Baker, former husband, self-employed children's entertainer, and part time pizza delivery man should die. The problem was how.

Vera knew there was no way she could do it herself. If she could, she would have done it years ago. She had perhaps missed a few opportunities, like the time they were at Harlstone Point. It would have only taken a hefty shove and he would have been in Davy Jones's locker, but the thought of failing and being tossed into the sea instead, had stopped her in her tracks. No, she would have to find another way. She would have to find an assassin.

This idea had its difficulties. Firstly, Vera suspected that hiring an assassin wouldn't be cheap and the stash of cash that she had kept secretly hidden in a shoe box in the attic was just a little over five hundred pounds. She hadn't the foggiest idea what the hourly rate might be and although the actual operation would, presumably, only take a few seconds she anticipated that the fee would include some sort of administration charges. She could at least wait a few more weeks until the children's entertainer, pizza delivery man and adulterer were back in England; that would at least cut down on having to pay a hired killer travelling expenses.

Money aside the biggest problem would be where to find someone prepared to do the deed. She could hardly put a postcard in the newsagent's window. Vera wasn't sure if Yellow Pages still existed but she couldn't imagine that they would allow criminals (professional or otherwise) to publicize their occupation. Although, Vera had noticed that there were more and more advertisements these days on the television for gambling and loan-sharks, but she guessed that particular form of 'robbing people blind' wasn't considered a crime.

Vera was contemplating whether it would be possible to search for a professional assassin on the dark web when, out of the blue, she had a bright idea. Why not employ an amateur? She felt sure that there must be some hard nut out there desperate enough to do the job for a few hundred quid. And in flash an image came into her head and for the first time in a long time she began to feel hopeful that her violent ex-husband would soon be out of her life for ever.

Vera approached the man with the dog with some trepidation. Despite not having had a square meal in months the hulk slouched against the Town Hall wall looked like he could strangle an angry gorilla with one hand. Undeterred, Vera stooped down and placed a manila envelope next to the dog's drinking bowl, and after making a courteous 'good morning', and suggesting that the contents of the envelope would be to the gentleman's advantage, she hurried away home and waited for the phone to ring.

Casper Alexander Pavlovsky, the gentleman in question and recipient of said manila envelope had not that long been awake and it took him a few minutes to take in what had just occurred. Suspecting, at first, that it was an official letter, from some authority or other, requesting that he crawl away and look untidy elsewhere, he was tempted to chuck it in the bin. He would have done so, had it not been for Ruby, his faithful wire haired Lurcher, giving him that 'don't be too hasty' look. On opening the envelope Casper discovered a telephone number but no name, a brief note offering him cash-in-hand for a day's work sometime in the near future and fifty pence in change for the phone call if he was interested in discussing the offer further.

Casper had been living on the streets long enough to know when something was not quite right, and he felt certain that the work in question would not be a simple matter of trimming the odd hedge or mowing a lawn. He had also learnt to recognise a troubled mind when he saw one and if he wasn't much mistaken the women who sped away so quickly had a lorry load of demons inside her head. Casper's own fragile state of mind was not awake enough to know what to do other than place the envelope in the front pocket of his rucksack and ask Ruby if she had any bright ideas.

Vera hadn't had to wait long for the phone call and now she was on her way to the Greasy Spoon Café at the bottom end of the high street to meet the man, who she now knew to be called Casper Pavlovsky and his dog Ruby. Vera had also learnt from the telephone conversation that the dog needed ant-inflammatory tablets for her arthritis and that was why Casper was willing to earn some extra cash.

"A lot of people say stuff about beggars spending money on booze; not me," he had said. "It's for Ruby. She's ten you know."

Vera hadn't known. And after he'd gone on about the cost of wormer tablets she was quite pleased when he had hung up.

Vera didn't recognise Casper at first, in fact if it hadn't been for Ruby she might have walked straight passed the table. He was closely shaven, wearing clean clothes, courtesy of the Salvation Army drop-in centre and to her surprise the newly scrubbed up gentleman, stood up the moment he saw her and pulled out a chair for her to sit down.

Three pots of tea, four toasted tea cakes, two glasses of John Smiths and a shared bowl of chips later they were still talking. Over the first pot tea Vera learnt that Casper's grandfather came to the UK during the Second World War and was one of a thousand or so Ukrainians, citizens of pre-war Poland, who joined the Polish Armed Forces under British command. To his great disappointment and sorrow, the stories he had to tell of the horrors of war did not deter his grandson from serving in the British Army. And so it was that after twenty years, two tours of Ireland and one in Bosnia Casper left the army behind for civilian life. A life he didn't know or understand. A life he feared and a life that eventually left him without family and friends.

And it was during the second pot of tea that Casper learned that Vera was an only child and promised herself that once she started a family she would make sure that it would be a big one. But as things turned out, she was glad that she didn't have any children. For as it so happened, her husband, William Baker, who went under the name of Mr Chuckles-a-Lot when he was entertaining children, maintained that he hated kids particularly the under-fives. Casper decided he didn't like Mr Chuckles-a-Lot a lot; in fact he didn't like him at all. And when he heard how the cowardly, nasty piece of work had left Vera, after a beating which had put her in hospital with broken ribs and a fractured collar bone he hated him.

By the time the last chip was eaten, Vera insisting that Casper should have it, the two people sitting in the Greasy Spoon Café knew a great deal about one other. It was only when Ruby got up and moved towards the door, indicating that she thought it was time to go, that Casper asked Vera "So what's the job?"

To say Vera was flummoxed would be an understatement. All thoughts of hiring an assassin, or killing her husband, had vanished.

"Shed!" she said a little too quickly, "I need the shed cleared out – all his stuff's there – don't want to touch it." and as if someone else was speaking she added, "It's not the Ritz but there's room for a single bed and it's got electricity."

She waited for Casper to say something and when nothing came she added. "There could be a problem if my husband came back and found you there. But what do think?"

Casper called Ruby away from the door and she obediently curled up once again under the table and Vera waited until two mugs of coffee were placed in front of them before saying "Well?"

Casper looked at Ruby and then at Vera"

"Yes" he said, adding with a reassuring, "And if Mr Chuckles-a-Lot comes back causing trouble, I could always kill him."

About the Author

Anne Bainbridge was born in Ilfracombe and has lived most of her life, in North Devon. She trained as a secondary school teacher, although she has taught students of all ages both in the classroom and the community and still teaches occasionally in a local primary school.

She has a B. Phil. Ed. and an MA in English - Film Study Pathway, as well as taking a creative writing module at the University of Exeter.

She cannot remember a time when she wasn't making up stories in her head, at night to bring on sleep or in school to dispel boredom. Making up stories for her children gave her the opportunity to fulfil her love of storytelling.

This book is the realisation of a long-held desire to put some of those stories into print to be enjoyed by a wider audience.

Before you go...

We hope you enjoyed this book and would love to hear your views, either directly, or on our website where you can write a review.

www.bluepoppypublishing.co.uk

Blue Poppy Publishing works with a number of authors, predominantly from Devon, helping them to publish and distribute their books.

Coming Soon

Inspiration

A collection of short stories by Anne Beer, another Devon based writer. Her stories, both true stories about her life, and fictional ones on a range of topics, will take you through every emotion. Written as a series of writing prompts over several years; members of the writing group she attends monthly felt they needed to be shared with a wider audience and she has finally been persuaded to allow them to be published for others to enjoy.

A Breath of Moonscent

A true story of a London child growing up in the wilds of Devon in WWII

A lyrical memoir of wartime and post-war rural Devon seen through the questing eyes of a young boy.

"*Allan Boxall portrays in words what Ravilious achieved in images.*" Liz Shakespeare.